Garre   nanny.

Whatever   ications were, she was absolutely wrong for the job. She belonged in the nursery of a Victorian home in San Francisco where she could use her skills on little rich kids.

How could the agency have sent her?

He noticed the shape of her long legs, her dark shiny hair falling against her cheek and the outline of her breasts under her T-shirt. It was fortunate that he had sworn off women after his painful past.

What was it about this woman that made Garrett tighten up inside whenever he looked at her? Which brought him to the real reason she couldn't stay. He found her too attractive in a way that could make things very awkward. The sooner he got rid of her, the better.

Dear Reader:

Happy holidays! Our authors join me in wishing you all the best for a joyful, loving holiday season with your family and friends. And while celebrating the new year—and the new decade!—I hope you'll think of Silhouette Books.

1990 promises to be especially happy here. This year marks our tenth anniversary, and we're planning a celebration! To symbolize the timelessness of love, as well as the modern gift of the tenth anniversary, each month in 1990, we're presenting readers with a *Diamond Jubilee* Silhouette Romance title, penned by one of your all-time favorite Silhouette Romance authors.

In January, under the Silhouette Romance line's *Diamond Jubilee* emblem, look for Diana Palmer's next book in her bestselling LONG, TALL TEXANS series—*Ethan*. He's a hero sure to lasso your heart! And just in time for Valentine's Day, Brittany Young has written *The Ambassador's Daughter*. Spend the most romantic month of the year in France, the setting for this magical classic. Victoria Glenn, Annette Broadrick, Peggy Webb, Dixie Browning, Phyllis Halldorson—to name just a few!—have written *Diamond Jubilee* titles especially for you. And Pepper Adams has penned a trilogy about three very rugged heroes—and their lovely heroines!—set on the plains of Oklahoma. Look for the first book this summer.

The *Diamond Jubilee* celebration is Silhouette Romance's way of saying thanks to you, our readers. We've been together for ten years now, and with the support you've given us, you can look forward to many more years of heartwarming, poignant love stories.

I hope you'll enjoy this book and all of the stories to come. Come home to romance—Silhouette Romance—for always!

Sincerely,

Tara Hughes Gavin
Senior Editor

CAROL GRACE

Make Room
for Nanny

Silhouette *Romance*

Published by Silhouette Books New York

America's Publisher of Contemporary Romance

To my father, who taught me to love books by reading to me every night when I was a child, and to my mother, who believes I can do anything I want to do

AUTHOR'S NOTE
All of the characters in this book are fictitious except for Big Lou, who is a real fish in a real pond and, as far as I know, is still at large.

SILHOUETTE BOOKS
300 E. 42nd St., New York, N.Y. 10017

ISBN: 0-373-08690-3

First Silhouette Books printing December 1989

Printed in the U.S.A.

CAROL GRACE

has always been interested in travel and living abroad. She spent her junior year in college in France and toured the world working on the hospital ship *Hope*. She and her husband spent the first year and a half of their marriage in Iran, where they both taught English. Then, with their toddler daughter, they lived in Algeria for two years.

Carol says that writing is another way of making her life exciting, and she often writes on the deck of her mountaintop home, which overlooks the Pacific Ocean and which she shares with her inventor husband, their daughter, who is now twelve years old, and their eight-year-old son. Carol is proud that writing runs in her family. Her daugher has had three stories published in her school magazine, and her son pens mysteries in his spare time.

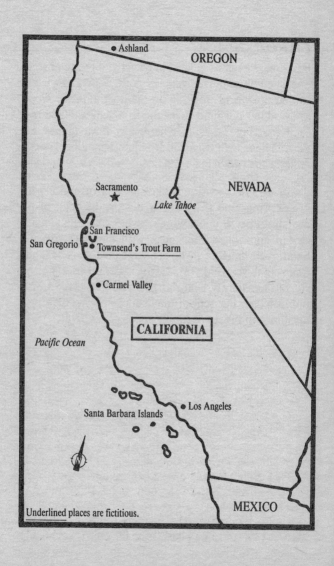

Ashland

OREGON

Sacramento ★

NEVADA

Lake Tahoe

San Francisco
San Gregorio · Townsend's Trout Farm

Carmel Valley

CALIFORNIA

Pacific Ocean

Santa Barbara Islands

Los Angeles

Underlined places are fictitious.

MEXICO

Chapter One

To say that Maggie was disappointed with the looks of her new employer was putting it mildly. "See the world with the rich and famous," they had promised her at nanny school. The man standing on the front porch of the dilapidated farmhouse seemed neither rich nor famous, and the disappointment in his face matched her own. On closer inspection, it wasn't so much disappointment as downright hostility. Dark, smoldering eyes glared at her from under a shock of brown hair.

She smoothed her gray skirt and held her chin high above her crisp white blouse. "To feel like a nanny, dress like a nanny," Mrs. Newcastle had advised her girls. At twenty-eight Maggie had been considered a girl by the older woman, though Maggie was confident she didn't look like one today. She stepped briskly out of her car and planted her sensible shoes firmly on the wide redwood planks that led to the house.

The man loomed on the front porch above her, broad shoulders in a rumpled plaid shirt, his hands on his hips.

"Mr. Townsend? I'm Margaret Chisholm, your new nanny." She held out her hand, but he didn't take it. His nostrils flared, and she almost expected him to breathe fire.

"I'm afraid not," he said curtly. "Our nanny is sixty-seven years old, and her name is not..." he paused, unwilling to even repeat her name, "whatever you said."

For the first time since Maggie had received her assignment from the computerized match-up program the day of graduation at Mrs. Newcastle's School for Nannies, her confidence faltered. "But I have my printout with me," she insisted, fumbling in her shoulder bag and digging for the envelope.

"So do I, and you don't fit the description." He spoke with quiet determination while he looked her up and down from the tips of her brown walking shoes to the top of her shiny, straight brown hair.

Maggie knew it might not be apparent at first glance, but if anyone was made for taking care of children, it was she. She'd been preparing for it all her life. She had taken the Red Cross baby-sitting class when she was eleven, clipped articles on natural childbirth when she was eighteen, and majored in home economics in college.

Right on schedule she got married at twenty-one and settled down to have a big, happy family. Unfortunately her family wasn't big or happy. She had three miscarriages in three years. The first one she dismissed as bad luck, the second depressed her and the third she accepted as fate. She and her husband grieved in their separate ways, and finally they did everything in their separate ways, and got a divorce.

Putting aside her aching sadness, Maggie convinced herself she was meant to care for other people's children, and she was to start right here with the six-month-old son of this towering ogre, Mr. Garrett Townsend.

After taking a tour of her with his eyes, Garrett finally met her anxious gaze and shook his head slowly but firmly. "I'm sorry you drove all the way out here, but it won't work. You just won't do."

The collar of Maggie's starched blouse was beginning to dig into her neck, and perspiration dripped down her back. She'd been driving for six hours in her nanny outfit, and she was afraid the match-up form wasn't in her purse, after all.

"What won't work? Why won't I do? I assure you I can do everything. You'll see for yourself when Mrs. Newcastle sends my transcripts and my recommendations." Maggie took a step forward and regarded him earnestly. "Just for starters I change diapers, cure colic and make formula. I know CPR and I have my Water Safety Instructor certificate." She paused, suddenly out of breath.

Garrett Townsend was staring at her, his mouth twisted in what might have been a grudging smile.

"That's all?" he asked, stuffing his hands in his back pockets, his eyes mocking her.

Maggie closed her eyes for a moment. Even if he was going to send her away, wouldn't it be common courtesy to ask her to sit down for a minute on one of those wicker chairs on the porch and offer her a glass of water? She licked her dry lips. If it wasn't for the baby she'd been sent to take care of, she would have walked back to her car right then and there and told Garrett Townsend what he could do with his job.

As if he'd read her mind, he motioned to a chair on the porch.

"Sit down," he ordered her brusquely. "I'll get you something to drink before you start back."

As he turned on his heel she caught him with her question. "May I see the baby?"

He froze, but he didn't turn around. "Baby? There is no baby."

Her chest heaved and she tried to catch her breath. "What happened to the baby?"

He braced his arms against the door frame. "He grew up," he explained patiently before retreating to the kitchen. "He's six years old now."

"But it said on the form…" Maggie was certain there was a "6" in the blank where it said "months old," but when she tried to picture it she couldn't. Instead she stared un-seeing at the dry fields that formed a valley between green, forested hills. So there was no baby. No baby, no job, no nothing to go back to, either. All the jobs were taken. All the graduates were matched up. She sank into the wicker chair and tightly gripped the arms.

When he returned she accepted the glass of water from his large, strong hands and drank it gratefully without looking at him.

"I'm sorry for the mix-up," he said almost civilly. "But I need someone older and more mature."

Maggie sat up straight and hardened her gaze. More ma-ture? That did it. She would not beg for this job. She didn't want it, anyway. Who in her right mind would work for this man? She looked him over to reinforce her determination. First the wrinkled shirt, sleeves rolled up above the elbows showing muscular sun-browned arms. Then narrow hips in tight, faded jeans that were ripped at one knee. Finally socks that didn't match and scuffed running shoes.

Which led to the big question. Where was the mender of jeans, the pairer of socks? Where was Mrs. Townsend? Or wasn't there any? He caught her staring at him, and she blushed.

"I understand," she said with all the composure she could muster. "You wanted someone older and I wanted some-one younger, a baby. Don't worry. Mrs. Newcastle will straighten everything out, and I'll find another family." When she stood up, he looked so relieved she almost laughed. *I must have given him quite a scare. Am I really that threatening?*

A phone rang somewhere in the house and Garrett Townsend looked almost euphoric. He couldn't have planned it better, she thought. She knew better than to of-fer her hand again, but to her surprise, he reached out and grabbed it.

"Goodbye, Miss . . . Mrs. . . . ."

"Chisholm."

"Right." He bounded into the house and when she heard the phone stop ringing she walked slowly to her car. Leaning against it was a small boy with straight blond hair and large glasses that made him look serious and wise.

"Hi," she said to him.

He looked up from the stick he was carving with a Swiss Army knife and took her in with his solemn gaze. Was she about to disappoint still another member of the family? She couldn't take much more of this. But he smiled at her with satisfaction.

"You look just like her. I knew you would."

So that was it. She looked like his mother. No wonder Garrett Townsend didn't like her. Too many memories.

"Who?" Maggie asked and held her breath.

"Mary Poppins."

She smiled with relief. "I have a big umbrella, too, just like hers."

His eyes were large, round and blue. Was this boy really the son of that disagreeable, misanthropic, rough-edged man?

"Did you bring that medicine that tastes so good?"

"Well, no I didn't. How do you know about Mary Poppins? Did you read the book?"

"Uh-uh, I saw the movie."

"Elliott," the man's voice came from the porch. Elliott retracted the blade of his knife and ran up the steps.

Unwilling to have further words with her almost-employer, Maggie opened her car door and sat behind the wheel. She peered out the window, wondering how Garrett got along with his son. They were sitting together on the top step of the porch and Garrett was talking earnestly while the boy nodded. She felt a stab of envy at their closeness.

Maggie started her engine. She had to get out of there before the September heat and the frustration and the fatigue got to her. Throwing the gearshift into first, she looked up to see Garrett Townsend standing in front of her car, his arms outstretched.

"Wait," he shouted. He put his head through her open window and frowned at her. "I told you you couldn't stay."

She wiped the perspiration from her forehead. "I know," she seethed. "I'm trying to leave."

He continued as if she hadn't spoken. "But I have a problem. That was my realtor up in the foothills. Some land I've been looking for has just come on the market. I'd like to go up there tomorrow, but Elliott has school and I can't take him with me." He stared at her intently.

He's trying to ask me to stay, she realized, but he doesn't know how. He only knows how to give orders.

"I'm not asking you to stay," he said, again reading her thoughts. "It's just for a few days, until I get a good look at the place." His face was so close she could see that there were creases around his eyes and she could feel his warm breath on her cheek. She gripped the steering wheel to keep her hands from shaking.

He was the most irritating man she'd ever met and she'd be damned if she'd stay here for another few minutes, let alone a few days. She looked at Elliott sitting on the top step, then back to his father, whose forehead was now furrowed with deep lines.

"Okay," she heard herself say. "If it's just for a few days."

He nodded. If he was relieved to hear her decision, he didn't show it, but he did open the car door for her. She followed him back to the house in awkward silence.

It was a relief to get out of her nanny clothes and into knee-length culottes and a short-sleeved T-shirt, although Mrs. Newcastle might not have approved. "It breaks down the barriers between employer and employee," she had said. But she hadn't ever met Garrett Townsend, who had invented the barriers between employer and employee. And it was so hot.

It was Elliott who showed her to her room, or rather the sixty-seven-year-old nanny's room on the second floor next to his, and the trout pond. It was Elliott who was trying to teach her how to cast, when his father ambled out across the field behind the house.

Garrett Townsend watched the nanny swing the fishing pole over her head, and shook his head as she failed to throw it out far enough. The line dropped about two feet away from the edge. Whatever her qualifications were, she was absolutely wrong for this job. She belonged in the nursery of a Victorian house in San Francisco where she could use her CPR and her WSI on little rich kids.

How could the agency have sent her out here by herself? He could have been a sex maniac for all they knew.

If he'd been a sex maniac, he would have noticed the shape of her long legs and her dark shiny hair falling against her cheek, and he wouldn't have been able to keep his eyes off the outline of her breasts under her T-shirt. It was fortunate that he had sworn off women after the painful separation from Helena.

Elliott laughed at the newcomer's clumsy attempts to land the line in the center of the pond. It was hard to believe that last summer he had never laughed at all. Garrett blamed Helena for that. He'd do anything to keep anyone from hurting his son again. Since the split, it was he and Elliott. And it was working out fine, just fine.

Unaware of his presence, the nanny bent over to look into Elliott's bucket of worms. What was it about her that made Garrett tighten up inside whenever he looked at her? Which brought him to the real reason she couldn't stay. He found her too attractive in a strange way and that could make things very awkward. The sooner he got rid of her, the better.

"Dad!"

They both turned to look at Garrett and he blinked, pushing all thoughts about the nanny to the back of his mind.

"Maggie can't do it right. You show her."

He walked over to them. So that was her name. Her face was flushed and tiny beads of perspiration stood out on her upper lip.

She eyed him warily and he didn't blame her. He'd been nothing but harsh since he saw her get out of the car. He'd been expecting a sweet, little old grandmother and instead he got...he got this Maggie. He'd been too disappointed to be diplomatic, and now, seeing her up close in that T-shirt and skirt-like thing, and the shock of her long, smooth legs so close to him left him feeling something more disturbing than disappointment.

"It's all in the wrist," he told her evenly. She looked surprised that he wasn't critical.

There was a damp spot on her T-shirt between her breasts, and he forced himself to look at her wrists. "Here." Before he could stop himself he picked up the pole and wrapped her hand around it. Then he stood behind her and put his arms around her, the fragrance from her hair making his heart pound so loudly he was afraid she'd hear it. He covered her hand with his and they swung the pole back together in one easy motion.

For a split second the line hung suspended over the water, then it sunk into the gray-green depths of the pond. He dropped his arms.

"Thank you," she said breathlessly.

Elliott clapped his hands in approval. "That was good, Maggie."

Garrett wanted to echo, That *was* good, Maggie, but he stalked back to the house instead, muttering instructions to himself. "Keep your eyes on her face, if you have to look at her, and keep your hands to yourself. No more lessons."

Despite the "Everyone Catches One" slogan on the billboard at the entrance to the farm, Maggie didn't catch one. The trout they had for dinner were caught by Elliott and they were delicious. Maggie offered to cook, hoping she could show Garrett she was good for something, but he coolly declined. He rolled the fish in cornmeal and pan-fried it with potatoes. He sent her and Elliott out to an overgrown garden to pick squash, which he cooked in another pan and sprinkled with Parmesan.

"Elliott knows what to do about the fish." Garrett spoke only after they'd finished eating and Elliott had gone outside to play in the last rays of autumn sunlight. "We feed them once a day. If anyone wants to fish, tell them they have to bait and clean them themselves until I get back." He was standing at the stove with his back to her, pouring hot water through a coffee filter.

She wished he'd look at her when he talked to her—or any time, for that matter. He seemed determined to treat her like the servant she was, or worse, like some unexpected relative he couldn't get rid of.

From the way he cooked and made coffee she guessed he'd been on his own for a while. How long had he been divorced or separated or widowed? From the way he acted, it was surprising that he'd ever gotten along with anyone long enough to produce a child.

He turned around, holding two cups of coffee and looking down at her; a quizzical look was in his dark eyes. She stood up and brushed her hair back from her face. Was it only a minute ago she wished he'd look at her? Now that he was, it made her uneasy. "It's so warm in here I think I'll take my coffee out to the porch," she decided.

He shrugged as if it didn't matter to him if she took it to the moon, but he held the screen door open for her and sat in the porch swing while she took the wicker chair. She felt the silence between them stretch endlessly, broken only by the squeak of the swing and the chirping of the crickets. The dark hills across the valley stood against the pale evening sky.

"Tell me, Maggie." The unexpected sound of his deep voice and the unexpected use of her name startled her so much she almost dropped her cup. "What made you want to be a nanny?"

How could she answer the question without confessing she'd failed as a wife and mother? How could she admit she wanted a baby so much it hurt her with a dull ache every time she saw one?

She steadied her hand. Garrett's face was shadowed by the awning, and she hoped hers was, too. "For the opportunities," she said finally. "To see the world. Some of the graduates spend summers in Aspen and winters in Gstaad. It can be a very rewarding experience."

"Financially." His voice was heavy with disapproval.

"Of course." She kept her voice light. So he sneered at money as he did at everything else. "What made you want to be a . . . a . . ."

"Marine biologist? I like fish." With that he closed the subject and the conversation and walked down the front steps in search of Elliott.

Later that night, after Elliott was asleep and Maggie had gone to her room, Garrett dumped a drawer full of unanswered letters and receipts on the kitchen table. He set a jar of peanut butter on top of the pile to keep them from blowing away in the warm evening breeze.

The stairs creaked and he looked up. When they creaked again, he stood and walked to the staircase. Maggie was standing on the bottom step in a long, white cotton robe that billowed around her.

"Oh," she exclaimed softly, "I thought everyone was in bed." Her face was pale in the semidarkness, and he almost reached out to touch her to make sure she was real.

She looked over his shoulder. "I think I left my purse down here." She brushed past him and the scent of flowers that followed her filled his senses with an unexpected longing. He watched her bend over to look behind the overstuffed chair, and saw her wide smile as she held up the large shoulder bag.

"I'm still looking for my letter from the agency," she explained.

"So am I, I'm looking for mine. I wanted to show it to you just so you wouldn't think it was anything personal. Just because your first assignment doesn't turn out right is no reason to feel you're a failure."

"No, I don't. It's just that I could have sworn . . ." Maggie's voice trailed off as she sifted through the purse's contents.

"You'll never find it that way." Garrett took the bag from her hands and set it on the table beside the mess of papers. He waved his hand toward the chair opposite him, but he couldn't tear his eyes away from her. It must be the robe that transformed her from a sensible nanny to some ethereal creature of the night.

She accepted his invitation to sit down, then emptied her purse in front of her. Garrett sat down again, but instead of going through old bills and cancelled checks he looked at Maggie. He noticed how her hair shone in the light from the hanging lamp, and he watched her fingers smooth wrinkled papers. It occurred to him that they might sit there all night going over and over the situation. Her eyelashes made shadows across her cheeks until she looked up suddenly and caught him staring at her.

"Here it is." She unfolded a large computer printout just as he put his hand on one that matched it. He stood and leaned over her shoulder. The smell of flowers hit him again, an old-fashioned bouquet—lavender and jasmine and roses—and he had trouble focusing on the form she held up in front of him.

"You are Garrett Townsend and this is your address, isn't it?"

He nodded his head, his senses overwhelmed by the nearness of her.

"I knew it," she exclaimed. Her finger traced a line down the page. "Age of child or children." She stopped suddenly. "Oh."

"What's wrong?" His voice sounded too loud to his ears.

"It does say six, but not months. You're right, he's supposed to be six years old, not six months old." She turned her face to him, only inches away from his and he saw a small worry line etched between her eyebrows. Her lips moved as if she were practicing what to say, but no sound came out.

"Well, it's a relief to know that my son is really supposed to be six years old," he said with a half smile as he
walked behind her chair back to his place.

"Yes, but I don't understand. Mrs. Newcastle knew I
wanted a baby. She promised me a baby." She looked up.
"Have you found yours yet?"

"Yes, here it is. Aha, you see, the name is Shortwell,
Hilda, and the age is sixty-seven."

"Yes, Hilda was in my class. I wonder if she's got my
baby." She looked at him accusingly.

He held up his hand. "Don't blame me. I'm just as disappointed as you are. Maybe more so."

"I know that," she said. He noticed with alarm that her
lower lip was trembling.

"It's not your fault or mine," he assured her, "if that
makes you feel any better."

She was quickly stuffing things back into her bag—a
notepad, a comb, a package of mints and a wallet. Then she
put the bag over her shoulder and held her chin high. "No,
I don't think it does," she answered and walked across the
room.

"Where are you going?" he asked, suddenly worried that
she might just walk out of his house in the middle of the
night, just because of a mistake, and leave him in the lurch
after she'd already said she'd stay.

"To my room." She paused with one foot on the bottom
step of the staircase. "Or rather Mrs. Shortwell's room."
Her lips trembled again, and he crossed the room and held
her roughly by the arms.

"Look, I'm sorry about this mess. You're disappointed
and I'm disappointed, but it doesn't do any good to…to…"

"To what?" She seemed in control of herself now and she
regarded him with a cool look.

"To do anything rash. You can see why somebody my age
and my sex can't have somebody your age and your sex…"
He faltered again, hung up on the word and the implica-
tions of the word. She flushed, the color rising on her
cheeks.

"Of course I can. A person like you can't afford to compromise his position in the community. And I have my reputation to think of, too. A nanny has to be above reproach or she loses her authority and she can't do her job."

He almost smiled at her earnestness, but he was afraid of hurting her feelings. She might think he didn't take her seriously, and he wasn't sure how to take her, at all. He realized he was still holding her by the arms and that if he pulled her toward him and held her he would feel her body against his through the white robe. He dropped his hands so suddenly she blinked.

"I'll call the agency tomorrow and straighten everything out," he promised her.

"No, I'll call—it's my agency. I'm their graduate."

"I'd like to speak to Mrs. Newcastle myself."

"So would I." There was a determined look in Maggie's eyes that he was beginning to recognize.

"All right, we'll both call her. I'll wait until I get to Placerville." That way he could say what was on his mind. Maggie stared at him as if she knew what he was thinking.

"In the meantime, I appreciate your staying. It means a lot to me to have someone here I can trust, and who Elliott feels comfortable with."

"I feel comfortable with him, too."

"I can see that." He smiled and she smiled tentatively back at him.

"Good night." She turned and her robe, billowing out behind her, brushed against his arm lightly. She left him standing at the foot of the stairs, listening to her door close behind her.

As he threw his paperwork back into the drawer, he gave himself another stern lecture about who Maggie was and why she was there, and he promised himself that tomorrow would be different. He would keep his distance, physically and emotionally.

Chapter Two

In the morning the air hung warm and heavy over the valley even before the sun rose over the hills. Maggie watched helplessly as Garrett poured cereal into a bowl for Elliott, made sandwiches for his lunch and walked out to the road with him to wait for the school bus. She was allowed to tie Elliott's shoes, but that was all. Garrett paid no more attention to her than if she were an appliance. She felt even less useful than the old-fashioned range in the corner.

She followed Garrett out to his car the way the hired help is supposed to do to receive its instructions.

"Don't answer the door," he said frowning at the crisp red-and-white checked shirt that was knotted at her waist.

Maggie looked up in surprise. "Why not?"

"You never know who it will be."

"You will if you answer it."

"We're not expecting anyone. Just don't answer it."

She shrugged. The man was paranoid, on top of all of his other faults. He looked more presentable today in tan slacks and a clean but wrinkled blue striped shirt. There were lines between his eyes she hadn't noticed before. Maybe this was the first time he'd left his son with a stranger.

"Don't worry." Impulsively she put her hand on his arm. "I'll take good care of Elliott."

His eyes searched hers, and she realized she'd broken the code. She'd touched her employer and what was worse, she realized with a start, she wanted him to touch her. She stared at his lips, wondering how it would feel if he kissed her. Of all the activities forbidden to nannies, kissing was probably near the top of the list.

He tilted her chin with his thumb and leaned toward her. His features blurred and Maggie's lips tingled in anticipation. Then his head snapped back as if he'd suddenly remembered something very important.

"Don't forget to water the garden," he ordered before he jumped into his car and left her standing in the dust wondering what had happened.

What had happened was that she had very nearly made a complete fool of herself. She pictured herself standing in the driveway with her eyes closed and her lips parted, waiting...for what? She walked back into the house, washed the breakfast dishes, then attacked the kitchen floor. You know what, she told herself, scrubbing a stubborn spot on the floor. And you're very lucky it didn't happen. As self-sufficient as Garrett Townsend might be, there were still cobwebs in the corners of the rooms, she noted with satisfaction.

"Take that," she muttered as she knocked them down with the end of a broom, trying not to think about his face so close to hers that she was sure he had intended to kiss her.

She thought about calling Mrs. Newcastle to find out what had happened, but deep down she knew what had happened, and it really didn't matter anyway. She had promised to stay here for a few days, and she wouldn't break her promise even if Mrs. Newcastle could instantly produce a baby for her.

At noon she paused in the middle of the kitchen and looked around at her accomplishments. Clear windows to look out at the view of the surrounding hills. Clean lino-leum to slide her bare feet over as she walked to the closed door at the end of the hallway—Garrett's room. Shouldn't she wash his windows, make his bed and iron his shirts? That must be a part of light housekeeping.

She pressed her cheek against the smooth wooden door for a moment and then hurried back to the kitchen. She had to get out of the house for a while. The town of San Gregorio couldn't be more than a few miles away. She would go grocery shopping. They couldn't eat trout every day, could they?

She drove into town and parked the car. As she crossed the street from the post office to the general store, she had no illusions about what she was doing. She was going to pack a lifetime of motherhood into a few days. First she and Elliott would make ice cream in an old-fashioned wooden bucket with a crank, then she'd tell him stories and play games. Where were his toys and books, anyway?

When he got off the school bus that afternoon she asked him.

"They're at my mom's house," he answered, his small face turned up to hers, his blue eyes magnified by his glasses. "We didn't have time to get them."

Side by side, they walked to the house. Maggie put a plate of cookies in the middle of the dining table, poured them each a glass of milk and sighed with satisfaction. It was just the way she had imagined her life would be if only things had been different. She bit into a warm, soft cookie and chewed thoughtfully.

"Well, on Wednesday, if I'm still here, I'm going to buy you some books when I drive over to Santa Cruz. What do you like to read about?"

"Dinosaurs and monsters."

So much for Mary Poppins. "Do you want to make ice cream after dinner?"

"What kind?"

"What's your favorite?"

"Vanilla," he said, and went out the front door to swing on the rope that hung from the oak tree at the side of the house.

While she mixed bread crumbs and ground beef together for a meat loaf, she watched him swing. Maybe he didn't need any toys out here in the country, but wasn't there even time to get his books before he left? They must have been in a real hurry.

The ringing of the telephone interrupted Maggie's thoughts.

"Hello, Margaret." Mrs. Newcastle's voice was British and very proper. "I guess you realize by now that there's been a dreadful mistake. I knew I shouldn't have let them talk me into getting that computer. In twenty-five years I've never sent the wrong person to the wrong place. And now look what's happened."

"Did Hilda Shortwell get my baby?" Maggie asked.

"I'm afraid she did. Of course the family was surprised at first, and Hilda was quite taken aback. She told me in confidence that babies made her nervous, but what do you think? I just spoke to her and Hilda has absolutely fallen in love with that baby." She paused. "So that I hesitate to take it away from her."

Maggie's heart fell. "Of course, I understand," she managed to say. Maybe if she had a baby to fall in love with, she wouldn't have the time or energy to think about Garrett Townsend. She looked out the window at the boy on the rope swing.

Even if Mrs. Newcastle offered her a baby right this minute, could she walk out on Elliott?

"I take full responsibility, of course, Maggie, and I'm going to make it up to you. How are you getting along, by the by?"

"Fine, but it's not quite what I expected."

"A trout farm in the middle of nowhere." Mrs. Newcastle clicked her tongue. "I should think not. The computer meant to send Hilda there because she loves the solitude of the country, but it's not at all the place for a young, attractive girl like you.''

"It's not so much that…" Maggie trailed off. How could she explain that she hadn't expected an employer who was irritating, short-tempered, disapproving, and worst of all, she hadn't expected to be attracted to him in spite of all that.

"Maggie," interjected the school director, "you were my star pupil. I've never seen anyone take to infant and child care the way you did. I know I can count on you to do a thoroughly professional job wherever you are. But it hurts me to think of you in the backwoods somewhere without the baby you requested. And I want you to know that I'm working night and day to find your replacement."

"But where will I go when you find her?"

"My dear, if I only had a dozen of you to go around to the families requesting nannies. A job for you is not the problem. The problem is to find someone who is willing to take care of a six-year-old boy surrounded by trees and trout and miles from town. Have I described it accurately?"

Maggie carried the phone with her to gaze out the front window at the green hills across the valley. "It's not that bad," she said a bit defensively.

"Spoken like a real trouper," Mrs. Newcastle said approvingly. "Ah, the computer repairman has just arrived. But don't think that your future will be decided by a machine. I am taking charge of your file, and as soon as I have someone to take your place you'll be on your way to your proper destination."

"Thank you," Maggie said, suddenly exhausted by the conversation.

Because there was no book to read, Maggie made up a story for Elliott that night about how Mary Poppins slew monsters and tamed dinosaurs and finally floated off in the sky under her umbrella. When she finished, Elliott took off his glasses and put them on a shelf over his bed.

"Could we make that ice cream again tomorrow?" he asked, trying to keep his heavy eyelids open.

"Sure," she promised and he smiled sleepily. She fought off the urge to hug him. She sensed he wasn't ready for that, but he looked so vulnerable she could hardly resist.

The phone rang. She stood up from the edge of the bed and ran down the stairs. Without hesitating, she picked it up.

"This is Garrett Townsend," he said sternly. "I wanted to see if everything was all right. I was worried about Elliott. I've never left him with a stranger before."

Maggie pressed her lips together. "Elliott's fine, but he's asleep. It's eight-thirty."

"I couldn't call earlier. I was marking off the boundaries of twenty acres of prime riverfront property." There was excitement in his voice. She could almost picture him smiling, but it wasn't easy. He didn't smile much, especially at her.

"How's everything?" he asked abruptly.

"Fine," she assured him. "How are you?" she asked politely.

"I'm trying to get a hold of the county surveyor, but he can't come until Friday. If you don't have another job yet, I'd like you to stay until I get back."

"Well, all right." She might as well be earning some money until she heard from the school. "Is it nice up there?"

"It's got everything." His words burst forth as if he'd been waiting for her to ask. "The Stanislaus River runs right through year round. There's room for raceways and holding ponds. But it needs work, lots of work and a big investment of time and money. Have you heard anything definite from Mrs. Newcastle? I spoke to her this morning, and she assured me she would arrange everything."

Maggie looked around the kitchen as if the answer could be found on the spice shelf or in one of the canisters. "No, not yet. I mean she's working on it but she doesn't have anyone for you yet, as far as I know."

"Well, tell Elliott I'll call him tomorrow night before bedtime. And maybe before that we'll have some good news about your replacement."

After she hung up Maggie paced back and forth on the clean linoleum. She could understand why he was so eager to have her gone, but she wished it didn't hurt so much to hear him say it.

As he'd promised, Garrett called the next evening. While he spoke to Elliott, Maggie walked into the living room and studied the tiles above the fireplace.

"She's nice," she heard Elliott say and she smiled to herself. "She's kind of old, though, like Grandma." Maggie frowned. "She didn't teach us to read yet," he continued, "and my favorite part is recess."

Maggie smiled again and walked past the door. Elliott was sitting on the floor, his back against the wall, the telephone cord stretched taut.

"She's nice, too, but she doesn't know that much about dinosaurs," he said. Maggie paused in the doorway. "Dad, were there people on the earth when the dinosaurs were living? Maggie says there were. She says Mary Poppins was there then." His voice rose in disbelief. "She says Mary Poppins was stronger than a dinosaur."

Maggie opened her mouth to protest, then closed it.

"What's your favorite dinosaur, Dad?" Elliott listened for a moment. "Mine's tyrannosaurus rex and Maggie's is brontosaurus—he's a vegetarian." Elliott paused. "I don't think so, because she made some meat for dinner. I don't know what kind it was, but it was brown and it had some good gravy on it."

Then there was a long silence punctuated by "uh-huh" or "uh-uh." Maggie walked back into the living room.

When Elliott asked his father, "Do you think Maggie is pretty?" she opened the front door to get some fresh air.

"Me too," Elliott answered. "And her hair smells good, too, like flowers."

Maggie braced her hands against the door frame. Suddenly Elliott ran through the living room.

"My dad wants to talk to you," he said.

Maggie picked up the phone. "Dinosaurs lived millions and millions of years ago," Garrett Townsend said as if he were giving a lecture. "There were no men then. So no man has ever seen a living dinosaur."

"No man, maybe," she answered, "but one woman. Her name was Mary Poppins."

There was a choking sound, then Garrett cleared his throat. "Don't let your imagination run away with you," he cautioned. "I don't want Elliott confusing reality with fiction."

"He won't," she assured him. "He's a smart boy." Had Garrett really said she was pretty? She made teeth-brushing motions at Elliott, who nodded and went upstairs to the bathroom.

"I don't know what you see in brontosaurus," Garrett commented with mock seriousness.

"Brontosaurus? Well, he's cute. He lived near the water and he needed a lot of food because he was so big. Who's your favorite?"

"Triceratops. With the three horns."

"Oh." Was this the same man who'd just given her a lecture? How serious was he?

Suddenly she remembered the feeling of his hand on hers, her shoulders against his chest as they lifted the fishing pole together. She wondered where he was. She pictured him in a motel room stretched out on a bed with his feet up.

Garrett's voice was almost a caress when he said goodnight to her. She was so confused by the mixed signals he was sending, she could hardly concentrate on the story she told Elliott.

Garrett Townsend had never been lonely in his life. Not when he had spent summers on the boat fishing in Alaska. Not when he did his hatchery fieldwork on the Snake River or his research on the spawning habits of salmon on the

Columbia. Then what the hell was wrong with him now, that he had to call home every night? He told himself that he was worried about Elliott, but he knew by the sound of his voice that he was fine. Finer than he'd been in years.

Why did he look forward so much to talking to Maggie?

Why was he running up a ridiculous phone bill talking about dinosaurs? He didn't know why, but it wasn't because he was lonely. He didn't know the meaning of the word.

He got up off the bed in his motel room and drove back to his new property. He sat on the bluff overlooking the rushing waters of the Stanislaus River and thought about the house he could build there for himself and Elliott. The lawn would slope down to the edge of the water. Suddenly there was the image of Maggie superimposed on his vision of the lawn.

You've got to get rid of her, he told himself. There was no room in his life for a woman, especially one with a mind of her own. He had tried that. He decided to get on the phone tomorrow and call that agency again. He needed to get somebody, anybody, as long as it wasn't Maggie. It would help if she was over sixty.

"Mrs. Newcastle?" Garrett said as early as he dared call the next day. "Garrett Townsend calling."

Mrs. Newcastle lost no time in telling him how lucky he was. He frowned at the phone.

"Maggie, uh, Miss Chisholm is very nice," he assured her, "but—"

"Quite wrong for you, I couldn't agree more," Mrs. Newcastle broke in. "She's looking for a baby, you know, and I've found her one. The family has a lovely summer place at the Lake where she'll meet suitable people and mix with a young crowd. She needs a lighthearted atmosphere after what she's been through. That's what I told her. So if all goes well, your new nanny will be with you on Saturday and Maggie will be on her way to San Francisco to meet the Masons." She sighed happily. "Sometimes my job is so satisfying.'' He could almost hear her rubbing her hands together.

Garrett hung up and stood staring at the telephone. What had Maggie been through? Did she intend to leave without saying anything? Why hadn't she told him? He clenched his fists.

If she was so eager to get away, couldn't she at least tell him herself that she was leaving? He would have understood that it was dull for her on the farm. He stuffed his clothes in his overnight bag, checked out of the motel and headed for home. Didn't she realize that Elliott needed some stability in his life? He picked up the phone to call the well-digger, and told him to come on Monday.

Chapter Three

It took Garrett fifty miles to remember that Maggie's leaving was his idea. He had actually wanted, even insisted that she leave. Maybe he should give up the idea of buying a new piece of property right now. He and Elliott were doing fine where they were. They had a comfortable routine, a nice, steady life with no surprises, no ups and downs. A peaceful, predictable life, which was just what they wanted after Helena. Elliott felt secure, and so did Garrett.

It was just that if he had his own hatchery he wouldn't have to depend on other suppliers and he could do some genetic research that interested him. And the fast-moving rivers of California held a fascination for him. But this could be put off until a new nanny could be found. With Maggie around he had an uncomfortable feeling in the pit of his stomach that bordered on excitement. He was experiencing it now, as he thought about seeing her in a few hours.

It was different from the way he'd felt about Helena, he knew that. But how different? How good at making these important decisions was he? If it was just himself, he could take another chance with a woman. But with Elliott, he couldn't afford to, ever. Period. He gripped the steering wheel with determination. Maggie had to leave.

He drove through Oakdale and wished he had Elliott so he could take him to the Hershey chocolate factory there. He drove through Tracy and wished he had someone to take to breakfast there. But he drove all the way home without stopping.

He parked at the side of the house and took the porch steps two at a time. The smell of cinnamon and sugar hit him as he opened the front door, and he staggered backward as if he'd been struck.

Maggie stood in the kitchen doorway, her cheeks flushed from the heat of the oven and the surprise of seeing him there. He stared at her; a huge white apron covered her knees. He frowned at her long, bare legs beneath the apron.

"What's that smell?" he demanded.

"Baked apples. There were so many on the tree, I thought I'd use some."

"Did you think I wouldn't find out?" he blurted. "Did you think I wouldn't know?"

She wiped her hands on her apron. "You're not talking about apples, are you?"

"You know what I'm talking about." He glared at her. "You're leaving."

"Where did you hear that?" she asked, still reeling from his sudden appearance.

"Not from you. I had to call Mrs. Newcastle to find out."

She stared at him. "I haven't heard from her. She said she'd call me."

"I called to remind her that I was in a hurry, that I needed someone older and…you know what I mean. I haven't kept anything from you."

"Is that why you're so mad?"

"I'm not mad. I'm hungry." He looked over her head to the kitchen. "Are those apples ready?"

Maggie turned to go back to the kitchen, more bewildered than ever. If he wasn't mad now, she'd hate to see him when he was. Startled, she felt his hands on her shoulders, and he turned her around to face him. The anger was gone from his eyes, and there was a hunger there that had nothing to do with baked apples.

His hands tightened on her shoulders. She kept her hands at her sides, while her eyes locked on his. He smelled like the river, fresh and cool.

Suddenly he dropped his hands. "Are you leaving?" he demanded.

She gripped the edges of her apron. "I thought that's what you came here to tell me. Anyway, I think I'd better."

She backed into the kitchen and removed the apples from the oven, grateful to have something to do. He told her to leave, but his eyes asked her to stay. He was the most maddening man she'd ever met.

She put an apple in a bowl and poured cream over it. He sat down at the table and watched her take off her apron. She was wearing shorts; baggy, blue denim shorts that concealed the curves of her hips and grazed the tops of her knees.

She set the bowl in front of him and folded her apron carefully. "I'll miss Elliott."

So she was leaving. "He'll miss you," he said quickly. "I can tell on the phone that he likes you. You fill a need in his life since his mother is out of the picture. It's only natural." Was it only natural that she filled a need in his life, too? Natural, Garrett admitted, but not possible.

Maggie sat down at the table opposite him, her spine stiff against the back of the chair. "Do you mean that he's not going to see his mother again?" She felt her eyes sting with tears. If she were his mother, she wouldn't let anyone keep her from seeing him.

"She doesn't have room in her life for a child. She made her choice."

"He said he left without his toys and books." Maggie frowned at a scratch in the table.

"That's right. With my ex-wife, business comes first. Toys and books second, and children last. We couldn't get out of there fast enough to suit me. Things are back to nor-mal now for Elliott, but you can see why I don't want an-other change in his life, so..." Garrett was going to say, so you can leave and I'll stay home with him, but the words didn't come.

"Well, if Mrs. Newcastle says she's found someone for you, it will be someone you'll like," Maggie assured him, in spite of the hollow feeling in her chest.

"And I'm sure Mrs. Newcastle has found someone for you, by now. Someone you'll like." His voice was stiff with disapproval.

"I imagine they'll have a baby," she explained.

"I'm sorry I can't offer you one. Why don't you have one of your own, if that's what you want?"

Maggie stood up and went to the stove to make coffee. Her chest ached at the thought of the babies she'd lost. She swallowed hard.

"It's easier to take care of them if they're not yours. Then when they're sick or you're sick of them, you hand them back to their parents. That's the nice thing about being a nanny. And you're not tied down, you're free to leave whenever you want."

"Like next week," he said angrily.

She pressed her lips together and whirled around. "From the first minute I got here you've been telling me to leave. You told me I wouldn't do. You told me I wasn't mature enough. You think I'm not right for this job." He opened his mouth to protest, but she held her hand up and kept talking. "So I finally get the message and you act as if I'm running out on you. What do you want from me, Gar-rett?"

She realized in the silence that followed that she had never called him by his name before. She knew then that she'd passed a milestone and that she couldn't go back to the way things were before, when they talked by long-distance at night. She saw by the look in his eyes that he knew it, too. Her words hung in the air and her heart pounded.

Garrett leaned back in his chair and looked up at her. Her dark hair fell forward against her flushed cheeks. Seeing her here in the kitchen, looking as if she belonged there, he wondered how on earth he'd ever have the willpower to tell her to go. He ran his hands through his hair. Her brown eyes narrowed to slits and her mouth that had looked so soft a minute ago was drawn stiff and tight. She was waiting for his answer.

"I can't ask you to stay. It must be boring for you here. God knows it's not Lake Tahoe. But if you could stick it out a little longer, I'd appreciate it and Elliott would appreciate it. I'm not easy to live with, I know that, but I wouldn't be here that often. I'm going to get an independent appraisal of the property and meet with the owner, and make my decision on whether I should go ahead. Then you can be on your way." He took a breath and studied her face, wondering what she thought. For a second a hint of sadness flickered in her eyes, and Mrs. Newcastle's words came back to haunt him. He wondered what it was that she'd been through.

Maggie looked down at her shoes and gripped the back of her chair.

"And if you decide to stay," he continued, "things will be different, I promise. We'll set up some ground rules." Here was a way to get through this awkward situation. It was so simple he wondered why he hadn't thought of it before. Just a few rules.

She looked up and smiled faintly. "For you or for me?"

"For both of us," he said briskly, as if it were all settled.

"Mrs. Newcastle says families should have meetings where the nanny and the family can discuss things, iron out their grievances before they become problems."

"Mrs. Newcastle has thought of everything, hasn't she?" he asked with a mocking smile.

"She's raised five children of her own and I learned everything I know from her," she said defensively.

"Everything?" he asked, his eyes on her lips, in spite of his promise.

"Almost everything," she said. He saw the color creep up into her cheeks. "Now about the ground rules. I think there should be a rule against discussing anything personal."

"Good idea," he agreed readily. "We really only need to talk about Elliott and household matters. Rule Number Two," he continued, "no physical contact." Her flush deepened. "That's for me, of course." He had to remind himself that she was only staying for Elliott's sake. She was certainly not interested in him.

"Anything else?" he asked. "If not, I'll go check on the fish." He walked carefully around her and out the back door, eager to escape from the tantalizing smell of flowers that seemed to come from her hair, the warmth of the kitchen and the sight of her wide eyes whose color seemed to change with her mood. "If you think of something, we'll have another meeting soon." The screen door slammed behind him.

Maggie pressed her face against the screen and watched him lope down the path toward the trout pond. If only Mrs. Newcastle was here to tell her what to do about Garrett Townsend. The older woman would probably tell her to get out of her shorts and back into her long skirt and starchy white blouse, but they were too uncomfortable and it was too hot.

Maggie sat down and dialed Mrs. Newcastle, not to ask for advice but to tell her she was staying, just temporarily.

Elliott came home from school and was so excited to see his father that he talked constantly and Maggie was spared the effort of making polite impersonal conversation with Garrett. After dinner while Maggie was doing the dishes Elliott got out the Monopoly game.

"You said we could play if we had more people," she heard Elliott say to his father in the living room.

"I didn't mean Maggie," Garrett said in a low voice. "Maggie might not like Monopoly. Anyway it's not in her job description, I'm sure. Let's go out and play catch with the ball I brought you."

"It's too dark," Elliott protested. Maggie turned the water on in the sink to drown out their voices. But Elliott came into the kitchen to get her.

"Please, Maggie, please. We can never play Monopoly because Dad has to be the banker and everything."

"But Elliott, I don't know—"

He grabbed her hand. "My dad will teach you. My dad is really good at Monopoly. He always wins."

"Oh he does?" She hung her dish towel on a hook and followed Elliott into the living room. Garrett was sitting on the floor in front of the coffee table shuffling Chance cards. Childhood memories came back to her of railroads, hotels, mortgages and piles of play money.

"I hope you're prepared to lose your shirt, Maggie," Garrett said without looking up at her. He knew if he did, he'd look at her striped cotton shirt the way he had during dinner, noticing the way it was unbuttoned at the neck revealing the soft hollow of her throat.

She sat on the floor opposite him and he put fifteen hundred play dollars in front of her and fifteen hundred in front of Elliott. How like him to take her for granted.

"I'm not worried." She smiled at Elliott, whose eyes sparkled with excitement. On her first turn she landed on Connecticut Avenue and bought it. The second time around she bought the Pennsylvania Railroad and on her third turn she snapped up Kentucky Avenue.

"Maggie's on a roll," Garrett said to Elliott, as he handed Maggie her title card. He carefully avoided touching her fingers. "Are you sure you want to blow all that money so early in the game?"

"I don't know," she said looking down at the board. "I haven't played for years. I thought this was the way to do it." She watched his hands while he shook the dice, large hands with wide fingers. Not hands for playing the guitar but hands for wiping away a tear or just holding. She looked away.

Garrett landed in jail and stayed there.

"Why don't you just pay the fifty dollars?" she asked. "You can afford it. You haven't spent a penny."

"Only the rich and famous buy their way out of jail," he teased. "I'll wait."

He waited until he threw doubles, but by that time Maggie had added the B & O Railroad and Marvin Gardens to her holdings. When she drew a Community Chest card it said, "You have won second prize in a beauty contest. Collect ten dollars." They both looked at her.

Elliott was indignant. "You should have won first prize, Maggie. Don't you think so, Dad?"

Garrett was silent, looking her over as if he were the judge, trying to decide between first and second. Was he just abiding by their agreement not to say anything personal or didn't he think she was beauty-contest material, at all?

She held out her hand. "May I have my ten dollars, please?"

"Of course." He dropped the money into her palm.

Elliott yawned and Maggie stood up. "I'll make some popcorn," she offered.

"I'm not tired," Elliott assured her. "And I want to see who wins."

"Maggie's going to win, and I'm going to quit before she owns everything in town. Go up and put your pajamas on," Garrett said firmly.

The smell of popcorn wafted through the house and Garrett absentmindedly arranged and rearranged houses and hotels on the square green board, barely conscious that he was doing it. His mind was on Maggie. The old farmhouse wasn't the same since she'd come. It wasn't just the smell of good food in the air, and it wasn't just the sparkle in Elliott's eyes. It was as though the atmosphere was suddenly charged.

When Maggie came back into the room with a big bowl of popcorn he looked up at her and realized that she'd entered their lives with the suddenness of the autumn wind. They didn't know anything about her background, at all. She set the bowl on the table and sat down in a chair, tucking her legs beneath her and looking inquiringly at the staircase.

Garrett read her thoughts. "He'll be down for his popcorn when he gets his pajamas on." He put rubber bands around the Chance cards and folded the board in half. "You're good at this game, Maggie," he said casually. "Where did you learn to play?"

She reached for a handful of popcorn. "I was just lucky tonight. If you think I'm good, you should see my father."

"Maybe I should. Where is he?" Garrett knew he was pushing his luck asking personal questions, but she looked so relaxed, curled up in the overstuffed chair, that he took the chance.

"At home in Virginia with my mother," she answered.

"Playing Monopoly?"

She smiled. "Oh, I doubt it. You really need more than two." The smile left her face so quickly that he wondered if it had been there at all. She brushed her hand across her mouth as if she were brushing away an unhappy memory. What had he said to make her react like that?

Maggie was relieved to hear Elliott coming down the stairs. Her throat felt so dry the popcorn wouldn't go down. She stood quickly. Was it so much to ask of life to have a family? Before the tears of self-pity could fill her eyes she hurried to the stairway, ignoring Garrett's puzzled frown, and brushed past Elliott on her way up.

"Dad," she heard Elliott say, "why does Maggie have to go to bed so early. It's Friday night."

Before she could hear his answer she had closed her bedroom door behind her. But instead of giving in to her loneliness, she turned the lights on and picked up a stack of magazines she was saving for Elliott. Determinedly she marked articles on dinosaur digs, dinosaur cookies and dinosaur hikes while she lectured herself.

She told herself she was lucky to be there. She was lucky to have Elliott. She couldn't ask for a nicer child. But he's not yours, a little voice reminded her. He had his own mother and his own father. She was only temporary and the more attached she got to him, the harder it would be to leave. And she would leave. Garrett had made that very clear.

She felt her eyelids droop and the magazine slide out of her fingers. She turned off her lamp and undressed by the light of the full moon. Her window was wide open, but there was no breeze tonight. She pulled on a long T-shirt that grazed her knees, and lay down on her bed. Two sets of footsteps came up the stairs.

''Maggie's tired,'' she heard Garrett explain as they passed her door on their way to Elliott's room. The low rumble of Garrett's deep voice told her he was reading a story to Elliott and the sound was so soothing she felt the muscles in the back of her neck relax. If he were a little closer she could have heard the words. But if he were any closer she might not be able to stop thinking about him.

She heard Garrett say good-night to Elliott and she lay motionless, listening to him come down the hall. When he reached her room he stopped and she held her breath. Her heart pounded so loudly she gripped the edge of the mattress. But after an eternity, he walked on by and down the stairs.

She breathed a huge sigh of relief, which she was careful not to confuse with disappointment. She closed her eyes tightly, but the images wouldn't go away. Garrett sitting at the dinner table, looking at her when he didn't think she saw him. Garrett on the living-room floor shaking dice and making Elliott laugh.

Try as she would, she couldn't shake off the nagging questions that kept coming back to her. What if . . . what if she had put her arms around him when he held her by the shoulders, and had run her hands through his shaggy hair? If she had, would she still feel the way she did now? Dissatisfied, disappointed, vaguely depressed? Probably.

She could only have been asleep for a few minutes when she heard the tap on the door. Was it Elliott having a bad dream? She jumped up and opened the door.

Garrett put his hand on her shoulder. "Maggie, I'm sorry to wake you up, but I need you. It's the fish, it's too hot for them. They're all at the bottom of the pond." His eyes looked into hers, asking more questions than the spoken one. Would she come with him? She nodded and followed him down the stairs.

She paused in the living room to look for her shoes but they were nowhere in sight, so she shrugged and followed him to the shed behind the house. He filled her arms with bags of ice from the upright freezer.

"It may not be enough," he said, "but it's better than nothing." The moon was behind the tops of the tall oaks and Maggie stubbed her bare toe on the root of a tree.

"Ouch."

"Here, hold on to me," Garrett ordered.

"I can't," she panted from behind him. "My hands are full."

When they reached the pond, the water was inky black; the trout were so deep in search of cool water that it looked deserted.

After they'd ripped the bags open, Maggie followed Garrett around the pond, dumping ice in as they went. After five trips back and forth from the shed to the pond, the ice was gone. Trembling from exhaustion, Maggie stood next to Garrett at the edge of the water. Her bare feet were sore and coated with brown dust.

"Where are they? Why don't they come back up?" she asked anxiously.

"I think they will, but it will take a little time before it makes a difference. Wait, there's one."

The gray back of a small fish wiggled just under the surface and Maggie leaned over to look at it. Her hip brushed Garrett's.

"Don't fall in," he growled, his voice rough with concern, and he pulled her back against him with his hands on her waist.

"I won't." She leaned against his chest to support herself. She was wearing nothing under the oversized T-shirt and if he'd been too busy to notice it before, he must know it now. His hands moved over the soft fabric to her ribs under her breasts. He turned her gently around to face him.

The moon rose over the tops of the trees and illuminated her face.

"Oh, Maggie," he breathed.

The tenderness in his voice caught her by surprise and her heart did a somersault. He cradled her face in his hands and he studied her eyes, her nose and her mouth. "Elliott was right," he said. "You should have had first prize."

She shook her head. "It's just the moonlight." A slight breeze rippled the pond and she shivered involuntarily.

He ran his hand down her back and rested it on her hip. "You can go back to bed," he told her softly. "There isn't anything else we can do."

She took a careful step backward, knowing her knees wouldn't support her much longer, afraid she'd fall into his arms and let him hold her. "What about you?" she asked breathlessly. The whole world seemed to hold still. There was no sound, not even a ripple on the pond.

His gaze held hers for a long moment as he considered the question. His face was shadowed, but his eyes were clear and calm. "I'll come later."

She ran down the path to the house and the safety of her small room. Her heart pounded, and she couldn't understand why she felt so exhilarated and so let down at the same time. Tossing and turning in bed, she never heard him come in. Maybe he stayed up all night with the fish. She would never know, because she would never ask. She'd already asked too many questions.

When Maggie walked into the kitchen the next morning Garrett was flipping pancakes in the air to Elliott's delight.

"Try to land one on Maggie's head," Elliott suggested.

"No thanks," she said lightly, ducking and avoiding Garrett's eyes. The magic of last night was gone. Chalk it off to the moonlight, Maggie told herself sternly, but when Garrett turned his back to her she couldn't keep her eyes off of him. He moved as gracefully as a panther, from the stove to the oven, his broad shoulders turning as he fried bacon and heated syrup.

The smell made her realize she was hungry, and when he handed her a full plate she thanked him and took it to the table. His eyes were as bright as if he'd had a good night's sleep; she wished she felt as well as he looked. His smile was as bland as if she'd been a casual acquaintance who'd dropped in to say hello. Maybe it had all been a dream.

"Well, Maggie," he said, folding his arms across his chest, "what are you going to do on your day off?"

She set her fork down on the table. "My day off?"

"Yes. Mrs. Newcastle suggested Saturday, but if you'd rather have Sunday..."

"Saturday's fine," she said quickly, looking down at her plate. Fine, but unexpected. She realized she had come dangerously close to forgetting her place. She had begun to think of herself as one of the family, when just in time Garrett Townsend had done her the very big favor of bringing her back down to earth with a large thump by reminding her that she was only an employee with one day off a week.

Elliott poured syrup over everything on his plate. "Where are you going?" he asked.

She carefully cut her pancakes into one-inch squares while her mind raced. Where was she going? The room was suddenly very quiet. Garrett had finished frying bacon and there was no more sizzle to break the silence.

"Carmel," she decided in a flash of inspiration. One of her classmates at nanny school had taken a job with a family in the Carmel Valley. At graduation Doreen had shown pictures of vast green lawns, a swimming pool, a tennis court and two-year-old twins. Of course that was just their summer house. Doreen might be on her way to see the world right now.

"Carmel?" Garrett's brow furrowed. "That's a lot of driving for one day. I've been meaning to take Elliott to the aquarium in Monterey. We could drop you off on the way and pick you up later. Or are you staying overnight?"

Maggie took a bite of bacon and chewed thoughtfully. "No, I don't think so. When do I have to be back?"

He looked at his watch. "Technically not until nine tomorrow morning. Sunday's our busy day. Families with kids, old people, everybody wants to go fishing on Sunday. Of course I couldn't ask you to help, that's not in your job description." He gave her a disarming grin.

"Of course not." She didn't allow herself to grin back. After all, she was just an employee.

"But if you're here," he continued, "you might want to watch."

"Maggie could help me bait hooks, Dad." Elliott's eyes shone with importance.

"Bait hooks with worms?" Her voice rose in alarm.

"I'm expecting a flat of night crawlers from Watsonville. If I had worms I'd open up today, but of course . . ."

"I know—you couldn't ask me to do that, either." She shook her head in mock disgust and ran upstairs on light feet to get a sweater. She threw it over a white dress that was dusted with a print of tiny wildflowers. When Garrett teased her she felt less like an employee and more like one of the family, and a very warm feeling settled around her heart.

Garrett was standing on the front porch when she came down. He had changed into clean, unripped pants, a blue button-down shirt and socks that matched. Even his hair was combed. He followed her gaze with amusement.

"I wouldn't go to all this trouble for just anyone."

Her heart skipped a beat.

"But the Monterey Aquarium is rather special."

"So I hear."

"You've never been there?"

"No, this is all strange territory for me." All strange feelings, too, for a twenty-eight-year-old nanny—the rush of excitement when she met her employer's gaze, the funny flip-flops her stomach was doing at the thought of riding to Carmel with him.

"Too bad you can't come with us."

Her head spun. She could go with them. She hadn't called Doreen yet. But she couldn't go. She mustn't spend the whole day with Garrett and Elliott. She must not get attached to them.

She had to fight off the urge to grin back at Garrett, to study his clothes and fantasize about him kissing her. She would allow herself to ride with him to Carmel; how could she say no without being rude? But the reason she was going was to have lunch with Doreen and that's what she would do.

"That reminds me," she said, "I have to make a quick phone call." Fortunately Doreen was home. And although she had to take the twins to a birthday party in the afternoon, she could meet Maggie for lunch.

Directions in hand, Maggie got into the car next to Garrett. Elliott sat in the backseat, also in clean clothes and combed hair, two plastic toy soldiers in his lap. If he was surprised at going to Monterey, with Maggie along for the ride, he didn't let on.

"I'm supposed to meet Doreen at the Carmel Valley Farm." Maggie fastened her seat belt as they drove down the dirt road toward the highway. "I have the directions here."

"I know where it is."

Maggie turned in her seat. Garrett, the country trout farmer, at the Carmel Valley Farm? "Have you been there?" she asked incredulously.

"Once or twice. The Crab Louis is decent."

"I'll remember that." I'll also remember that Garrett has a whole life that you know nothing about. Dinners, lunches, vacations with his wife or somebody.

The sun had just risen over the hills across the valley, but the air was already warm. Maggie looked at Garrett's profile. He was looking straight ahead, and he smelled like fall, a warm, lazy smoky smell.

"I don't think I thanked you for last night." He turned and his face seemed so close to hers that the memory of last night at the edge of the pond rushed back. She would not allow herself to get caught in that trap again, expecting a kiss that never came. "The fish were back to normal this morning."

And so are we, she thought. "That's quite all right," she answered briskly and looked out the window. "It's all in a day's work. Man works from sun to sun, but a nanny's work is never done."

He frowned and concentrated on making a left turn onto the highway. "That sounds like something Mrs. Newcastle would say."

"Yes, it is."

Garrett suddenly regretted his impulsive offer to drive Maggie to Carmel. At home he could have cleaned the filters to keep from thinking about how Maggie had looked in the moonlight last night. Sitting next to her in the car for an hour and a half, it was going to be hard to erase the image of her features, pale and beautiful, as if sculpted out of white stone. She didn't feel like stone, he knew that much, and the moon was so bright he'd seen the outline of her breasts under the thin T-shirt that barely covered her knees.

When she'd turned to run back to the house, his eyes followed the curve of her hips and he'd forced himself to stay where he was and not follow her. He was only beginning to realize what a superhuman effort it was going to take to maintain this unnatural situation.

The obvious solution was for Maggie to take weekends off while he stayed home with Elliott. But when he tried to suggest that this morning, he heard himself offering to drive her to Carmel. Which was a terrible mistake, because the more he saw her, the more he wanted to see her. And now he was sorry she had to eat lunch with her friend instead of going to the aquarium with them. What would they talk about? Compare jobs maybe, and compare employers and children. Then Maggie might come back restless and dissatisfied. On the other hand, visiting the Monterey Aquarium was an enriching experience. One that he wanted to share with her.

Maybe she felt it, too. She hesitated in the parking lot of the restaurant as she got out of the car. "Have a good time," she told them through the open window.

Elliott suddenly leaned forward, his face screwed up in a tight frown. "Where's Maggie going?"

She bent down and looked at him through the window. "I'm going to have lunch with a friend of mine. She's a nanny like me."

"You said you were coming with us," he protested loudly.

"No, I said I was riding with you, but today's the day for you and your dad to do something together."

"Why?"

"Why? Because you haven't seen him all week. And this is my day off."

"Why do you have to have a day off?" he persisted. "We want you every day."

Garrett turned around. Even if it was true that they wanted her every day, he couldn't let Elliott continue to make a scene. "That's enough," he said sternly. "Maggie can't spend every day with us. She'll get tired of us." Garrett turned back to Maggie as if daring her to disagree.

Maggie looked around the parking lot. All she had to do was to find Doreen and explain that she couldn't get away and she could go with them.

When she looked back into the car, they were watching expectantly. She opened her mouth to speak, to say that she'd never get tired of them, that she wanted to spend every day with them. But she couldn't do that. She was a nanny, and this was only a job. She squared her shoulders.

"See you later," she said brightly.

Garrett wanted to shout, Get back in the car, you belong with us. Instead he said calmly, "I'll pick you up at four in front of the library in town. You'll probably want to look around." He was glad to hear his voice sounded sure, decisive, all business. All the things he didn't feel.

The wind blew her hair across her cheek and she nodded and waved. And he left her there, to go to the aquarium with Elliott and have an enriching experience.

Chapter Four

Doreen had to leave to get the twins before Garrett picked up Maggie, so she was sitting on the front steps of the library, surrounded by packages—little gifts she'd bought for friends and a big gift for Elliott.

"How was lunch?" Garrett asked, taking her packages from her and placing them in the backseat next to Elliott.

"Fine. How was the aquarium?"

Elliott leaned forward. "The otters are the best, Maggie. You should see them."

"I'd like to see some otters. You see that big box back there, Elliott? There's something in it for you."

Elliott's eyes widened in surprise and he quickly opened the box. She held her breath. Would he think it was too babyish? He held it at arm's length for a minute, looking it over, from the stuffed bear's ten-gallon hat to the leather cowboy boots. Then he looked at Maggie with a satisfied smile.

"I never had a bear."

"I didn't think you had one."

"You didn't have to do that." Garrett looked almost disapproving as he drove toward the ocean beach.

"I couldn't help myself," she explained.

"I thought we'd go home along the ocean, through Big Sur. It's slower, but it's more scenic."

She nodded and leaned back in her seat. They drove in silence and soon Elliott's head was resting on his new bear and he was asleep.

"How does your friend like her job?" Garrett's deep voice broke the silence.

Maggie looked at his profile. It wasn't like him to make polite conversation. "Doreen? Oh, she likes it fine. She's in love with her tennis teacher."

"I didn't know nannies were permitted to fall in love." Garrett took the curves of the coast highway slowly and allowed himself a long look at Maggie. "I thought that was against the rules."

"We're not permitted to fall in love with—I mean falling in love with your tennis teacher is okay, it's just your employer you're not allowed to . . . well, you know, it could be awkward." Maggie made an effort to keep her voice cool and impersonal, but she felt her cheeks burn as she saw his eyes gleam with amusement at her discomfort.

She turned her attention to the scenery. To their left sheer cliffs led to the pounding surf below and giant redwoods towered above them on the right. The sun hung low over the gray-blue Pacific, threatening to slide into the sea at any moment.

Maggie thought she'd never eat again after her large lunch at the Farm, but when Garrett suggested stopping at Nepenthe she realized she was hungry again. The restaurant was perched on the rocks hundreds of feet above the ocean with a view through the floor-to-ceiling plate-glass windows that made her gasp.

Garrett smiled at her reaction. They walked to a table next to the window. It was early for dinner, and there were only a few people at the bar. Elliott leaned against Garrett and finally put his head in his father's lap and fell asleep again.

Maggie pressed her hand against her chest as if to stop the aching loneliness she felt there. Maybe taking care of somebody else's child wasn't the answer, after all.

"Are you all right?" Garrett frowned at her.

"Fine. Just tired."

"The soup will fix you up."

The soup did help fix Maggie up, at least until she got back in the car. Then she too fell asleep with her head against Garrett's shoulder. She made an effort to pull herself up straight, but she dreamed that someone pulled her back to him. Was it Garrett?

When they finally pulled up to the farmhouse, crickets were chirping in the darkness. Maggie avoided looking at Garrett. After all her lectures about the proper behavior of nannies, how could she allow herself to sleep on her employer's shoulder? This was no way to establish her credibility.

She held the front door open as Garrett carried Elliott into the house and up the stairs to his bedroom. Then she quietly slipped into her own room without saying goodnight.

The kitchen was empty when she came downstairs the next morning in blue jeans and a T-shirt. She'd lain in her bed until she'd heard the back door slam. She was in no hurry to face Garrett. After all, he'd said she wasn't on duty until nine o'clock. But even as she ate her cereal she could hear cars arriving at the pond.

Finally at five minutes after nine, she forced herself to saunter casually toward the pond where a dozen or more people were already casting lines into the gray-green pool.

Elliott was baiting a hook for a boy not much younger than himself on the other side of the pond and he didn't notice her. But Garrett looked up from threading a worm on a hook to inspect her as he'd done on the first day she arrived.

"You're late," he remarked sternly, but his eyes held warmth in their brown depths and something else she couldn't define.

She looked at her watch and stifled a retort. "I'm sorry. Can I help?"

"Yes." She followed him inside the shack where piles of worms writhed and wriggled in buckets. She shuddered. "You can bait hooks, unless you're not up to it," he challenged.

"Of course I'm up to it," she assured him. "But what about the worms? Are they up to it? Doesn't it hurt?"

"A worm has no nervous system other than the ganglia that runs down its middle. The only point where a worm senses anything is at either end. So take the hook—" he picked up a worm in one hand and the hook in the other "—and thread it through like this."

Maggie winced and closed her eyes as the hook went through the middle of the worm. When she opened them, Garrett was standing so close to her she could feel his warm breath on her cheek. The expression in his eyes made her catch her breath.

"Something wrong?" he asked softly.

"I feel sorry for them, that's all," she admitted.

When Elliott appeared in the doorway, she reached down to hug him lightly, fishing pole and all.

He smiled at her, his eyes larger and more owlish than ever. "Dad, the people are waiting for you."

Garrett nodded. "I'll go clean fish. You bait hooks. Maggie will weigh and collect money."

Elliott raced back outside looking responsible and important.

Garrett put his thumb and forefinger under Maggie's chin and looked deep into her eyes. "All right?"

Maggie tried to cover her feelings of deep relief. "Sure. But I could have baited the hooks. Now that I see how it's done, and I know it doesn't really hurt them."

He shook his head. "It's really Elliott's job." His eyes crinkled at the corners, and she didn't know if he was laughing at her. At the moment it only mattered that she could turn her back on the buckets of worms and walk out into the sunshine to take her place at the scale and cash register.

It was a busy day at Townsend's Trout Farm. People streamed in and out of nowhere, children and even old people in wheelchairs. They each caught a fish. At the end of the day Garrett and Maggie and Elliott walked slowly back to the house. Maggie ran a bath for Elliott, and after he ate a bowl of soup he went to bed, his arm around his new teddy bear.

"I thought he might be too old for it," Maggie told Garrett. She was curled up on the couch, her head back on the cushions, too tired to move.

"You're never too old to want somebody to hug at night," he said, his back to her as he put another log on the fire in the stone fireplace. The fog had rushed up the valley, breaking the heat wave, and there was a chill in the air. Maggie looked at the back of his head, noticing the way his hair brushed the collar of his shirt.

Somebody to hug at night. Somebody with broad shoulders and dark eyes. If he turned and put his arms around her right now, what would she do?

Garrett turned to look at her, but she shifted her eyes to the flames. What a woman, he thought. She got up in the middle of the night and followed him out to throw ice in the pond without asking questions. She weighed fish all day and the only complaint she made was that she felt sorry for the worm. What was underneath that smooth, soft skin of hers? he wondered. Why didn't she have a husband and children to take care of? Why was she staying here for him? Was it just a job to her?

"I really earned my salary today, didn't I?" Maggie asked as if she could read his mind.

"More than that." He eased his long, lean body into the overstuffed chair at the edge of the fireplace. "If it weren't for Elliott, I'd take you out to dinner."

"If it weren't for Elliott, I wouldn't be here. Anyway you took me out last night. I shouldn't have let you—it's against the rules."

The corners of his mouth turned down. "I should have known. Then you'll have to eat hamburgers, cooked here over the fire."

He stood and looked down at her; her cheeks were pink from the warmth of the blaze. If her eyes had met his he would have taken her hands, pulled her up and held her to him, feeling her body against his. He willed her to look at him, concentrating on the soft, shiny tendrils of hair on the nape of her neck. But she stared deliberately at the fire.

Don't you feel it? he wanted to ask her. Or is it only me? Had he been alone too long or was this the real thing, at last? Even if it was, he cautioned himself, this was not the time or place. This woman, this desirable woman, was not for him. She was a nanny. His son's nanny.

"Fine," she murmured.

He turned quickly to go to the kitchen before he forgot the rules and Maggie had to remind him again.

After dinner he told her he would be gone all week on the Stanislaus River. "I'll be leaving early tomorrow morning. Will you be able to cope by yourself?" He stood in the middle of the living room with a cup of coffee in each hand; she stood to take one from him. Her fingers brushed his hand and the contact gave her a jolt that shook her down to her toes.

The coffee cup rocked on its saucer and she set it down on the mantel. "Of course," she said carefully, "as long as no customers come. Elliott and I get along just fine." She sat on the arm of the large chair that faced the fire.

"I appreciate what you did today," Garrett said calmly. It was obvious that he felt nothing for her but gratitude. "I can't imagine anyone else pitching in like that. It was above and beyond the call of duty. Most women would have just refused." He sat opposite her on the couch, looking at her steadily over the top of his cup.

Maggie took a deep breath. "Like your ex-wife?" she inquired. "Is she afraid of worms, too?"

He snorted. "Helena? She's not afraid of anything. But she wouldn't stoop to baiting hooks with worms. She's a deep-sea fisher, and she wouldn't be caught dead fooling with small stuff like trout."

"Oh." Maggie's shoulders slumped with disappointment. Somehow she had pictured Garrett's wife as being too delicate for this kind of life. Perhaps even the helpless type who read magazines and ate chocolates all day. If she thought she could outdo Helena by weighing a few fish, she was obviously wrong.

Garrett stretched his legs out in front of the fire. "Hauling in salmon day after day got boring for me. What I like is breeding and watching fingerlings grow. This land I found would be perfect. Twenty acres along the main branch of the Stanislaus. I've never seen so much fresh water. Low banks and shallow pools . . . you ought to see it."

He paused. "You ought to see it," he repeated. The thought of Maggie standing at the edge of the river and walking along the banks with him made his pulse throb.

Maggie rubbed her finger thoughtfully across her lower lip. "I'd like to but . . ."

"Yes?" He was ready to squash any objections she could come up with.

"When would we go?"

"On the weekend," he said quickly. "We could camp out on the property in our tent . . . tents. There's a meadow that's dry now, but in the spring it's green and there are wildflowers."

"I won't be here in the spring," she reminded him.

"We'll go now . . . soon. I want you to help me decide if there's a good site for a house. The realtor suggested the knoll for the view, but I'm thinking of building an earth-sheltered house into the side of the hill."

She smiled at his enthusiasm, but choosing a house site for someone was bound to stir up feelings of envy and regret, feelings unworthy of a first-rate nanny.

"I don't know," she said doubtfully, "I've never been camping."

"Never been camping?" He raised his eyebrows in mock horror. "So I've finally found something that Mrs. Newcastle didn't teach you. Good. I'll teach you, and Elliott will teach you. You'll love it."

Maggie smiled weakly and changed the subject. There would be time to back out later. "What are you going to do there that you can't do here?"

He stared at her. Get you to relax. Get you to stop thinking of yourself as a nanny. See you unwind. I can handle it, he told the nagging voice in his head. Up there I can be objective.

"Everything. I'm going to raise the healthiest, fastest-growing fish." He stood and looked down at her. "Don't tell anyone about this. So far it's just experimental."

"I won't," Maggie murmured, startled by the passion in his voice. "How are you going to do it?"

"Good question. By careful breeding."

Maggie wobbled backward on the arm of her chair, desperately trying to think of a way to change the subject. Garrett caught her arm and steadied her.

"There I go again, making scintillating conversation about fish." He grinned. "There must be something else we can talk about, besides mating." Instead of letting her go, he moved his hand up to her shoulder and to the back of her neck.

Maggie's brain raced, searching for a safe conversation topic, but she couldn't think of anything, couldn't think at all with Garrett's warm fingers on her neck gently moving down under her collar, blotting out all rational thoughts.

"What are you doing this for, Maggie?" His voice was low and his hand moved up to cradle the back of her head, his fingers caressing her hair. "I know what you want, and this isn't it. I'll never be rich and famous. But I wish I had a whole house full of babies for you to take care of. I would have liked that, but it didn't work out that way."

Maggie wanted to reach for his hand, to say that her life hadn't worked out that way, either, but the words stuck in her throat. She'd rather die than tell Garrett what a failure she'd been. She slid down into the chair and away from his touch. She forced herself to speak in a normal tone.

"How did you get interested in fish, Garrett? Did you grow up by a river?"

Garrett sat down on the raised hearth with his back to the fire and crossed his arms. Something he'd said had caused a curtain to fall between them. The more he opened up to her, told her about his doomed marriage and his hopes for the future, the more she withheld information from him.

And now she was asking polite questions, as if they were at a cocktail party instead of in an old farmhouse in front of a glowing fire with the fog hugging the house, separating them from the rest of the world. He wanted to pull her out of the huge chair that threatened to swallow her up, but he made himself stay where he was.

"I grew up across the Bay in Oakland, but my grandmother lived on the Columbia River. Her father owned a ferryboat and she called herself a river rat. We'd go up there when I was a kid and she called me that, too. I always thought it was a perfect place to grow up."

"And now Elliott will be able to grow up on a river like that."

"Yes. Where did you grow up, Maggie?" he asked softly. She surely couldn't refuse to answer a simple question like that.

"In Virginia."

"I can picture you there, in the Blue Ridge Mountains."

She shook her head. "It wasn't anything so colorful. It was a suburb of Washington, D.C. My father worked for the government, long hours, and I was an only child."

"It sounds lonely," Garrett remarked, and stared at her, willing her to go on. "So you decided to leave and become a nanny," he prompted.

Maggie sighed and stood. He saw her glance at the stairs and he wanted to hold his arms out, to stop her from going.

Stay, Maggie, stay. Tell me what happened. I need to know and you need to tell me, he silently urged her.

But Maggie yawned deliberately and there was no mistaking her intentions. "I'll see you in the morning before you go, won't I?" she asked.

He nodded, hating the day to end this way. Unfinished, incomplete, still full of possibilities. After she had gone upstairs he sat in front of the fire thinking how different Maggie was from Helena. Had he really said Helena was afraid of nothing? Nothing but tenderness, compassion and warmth. All of which Maggie seemed to possess in abundance. Before it had happened, he hadn't believed a woman could turn her back on her own child and never look back. But Helena had done it. It had shaken his faith in his judgment.

He had taken Elliott and they'd made a new life for themselves, a good one. And getting better by the day, thanks to Maggie. Maggie. What did she want from him, and what could he give in return? He went to the kitchen and poured himself a glass of wine. Then he slouched in front of the fire until the last ember died.

Maggie was relieved to see Garrett leave the next morning. There was nothing she could do on the farm that didn't involve him. Casting her line brought his arms around her. Learning to bait hooks became an excuse to stand next to him and to look into his eyes. Conversation that was supposedly about fish had hidden meanings. It wasn't safe to discuss anything, even teddy bears. She was conscious of his presence every moment, and if he hadn't left this morning she would have had to.

She was throwing dirty clothes into the washing machine when they called her from Elliott's school. Elliott had vomited there. Stomach flu was going around. Would she come and pick him up? She dumped the laundry on the floor and drove into town as fast as she could.

Elliott had looked fine that morning but he hadn't eaten much breakfast, now that she thought of it. When she saw him in the principal's office, his face was white and his lower lip trembled. She scooped him up and carried him to the car. He lay flat in the backseat with a stack of paper towels the school secretary had given him, just in case.

Maggie drove slowly. Looking at him in the rearview mirror, she asked, "How do you feel now?"

"Okay." He sat up and stared out the window. Was he really sick, or was there some reason he didn't want to go to school? When he rolled the window down and put his head out, Maggie knew that he wasn't pretending.

At home she put him on the couch in front of the television set. He looked up at her with a worried frown. "How can I feed the fish if I'm sick?"

She ran the palm of her hand across his cheek. "I'll do it. The food's in the shed, isn't it?"

It was a gray, overcast day and Maggie paused at the edge of the pond. The fish gathered immediately as if she'd rung a bell.

After she made a full circle, she went back to the living room to ask Elliott how he felt, but he'd fallen asleep. She removed his glasses and felt his forehead. He was warm, very warm. Garrett had left the phone number of his motel on the counter; Maggie dialed it and held her breath. When she realized that he wouldn't be there yet, she put the receiver down and paced back and forth across the living-room carpet.

Abruptly she stopped her pacing and picked up the phone again. This time she left a message to have him call her when he arrived. It's just the stomach flu, she told herself, but what if it wasn't?

Garrett didn't call until five in the afternoon and by that time Elliott had vomited five more times. In between Maggie had read him two stories and he'd slept for three hours. She pulled the phone over to the couch to let Elliott talk.

"Fine," he said in answer to Garrett's question, and Maggie smiled. "Well, I was sick at school during the pledge to the flag, but Maggie made Jell-O and ginger ale and I don't even have to eat dinner." He looked up at Maggie for confirmation and she nodded. "When are you coming home?....Okay....Okay....." He handed the phone to Maggie.

"Should I come home?" Garrett asked and her heart lurched.

"No," she said quickly, "he's getting better."

"You're not going to get sick, too, are you?" he asked gruffly. "You're the only healthy one left."

"Of course not. How's everything up there?"

"Terrible. The county just mentioned to me that if I was the guy who was thinking of starting some kind of fish farm, I'd better file an environmental impact report."

"But why? How are the fish going to impact the environment? It's their environment, isn't it?"

"You'd think so, wouldn't you? But instead of spending the day outside checking water levels, I stood in line at the county building and filled out forms." His voice got louder until she had to hold the phone away from her ear.

"What about tomorrow?"

"Back to the county building, more red tape, more forms, more bureaucracy." He paused. "Unless you want me to come home," he suggested. Maggie thought he sounded hopeful.

She gripped the receiver tightly. "Oh, no, no. I can manage just fine."

"I think I'd better come back."

"Come home if you want to, but we're getting along fine without you."

"Spoken like the perfect nanny." Garrett's voice was full of grudging admiration. "You really are something, Maggie. You've got magic in your medicine and magic in your touch. Do you know what I'm talking about?"

Maggie steadied her hand. "No," she said. "Not exactly. Well, I'd better start dinner."

"And I'd better go try to find something to eat in town."

"By yourself?" Maggie wondered if he hated to eat alone as much as she did.

"No, I'm having dinner with the planning department. Of course I'm eating by myself. I don't know anybody but the people I met today, and I wish I hadn't met them."

"Maybe tomorrow will be better," Maggie suggested, then winced. She was starting to sound like Pollyanna.

"No, it'll be worse. You haven't seen these guys. They're out to get me. To bury me under a pile of paperwork, to tie me up in red tape so that I can't have my hatchery."

"Are you going to let them do that?"

"After I've spent half my life looking for this place? I'll stay here and fight until I've filled out every form in the whole county." He paused. "Unless you need me. Are you sure you don't need me there?"

"Garrett, I'm a graduate nanny with honors. I've been trained to handle emergencies."

"I'll see you on the weekend, then."

Maggie stood staring at the phone for a long moment. Was that disappointment she heard in his voice? Was she wrong in telling him not to come?

When Garrett called the next night he talked to Elliott and didn't talk to Maggie. He was afraid if he did he'd try to talk her into saying he ought to come back. The next night he called again and carefully avoided talking to her.

Garrett walked away from the pay phone in front of the diner on Main Street. Elliott was getting well, but something else wasn't getting well, at all. He had tried talking to Maggie on the phone, he had tried not talking to her. But nothing relieved the pressure he felt to see her.

He walked up Main Street slowly, looking in windows without seeing the hardware and farm equipment inside. Instead he saw the farmhouse with Maggie inside. He pictured her putting Elliott to bed and curling up on the couch in front of the fire. He stuffed his hands in his jacket pockets and shook his head at his reflection in the window of the corner bakery.

You idiot, he scolded himself. You could talk to her in person. She was only one hundred and seventy-five miles away. All he needed to do was to get into his car and put his foot down on the gas pedal and drive for three hours.

He ran his hands through his hair and he crossed the street. He couldn't drive back and forth across the valley just to say hello to Maggie in person. Besides he had a meeting tomorrow at one in the afternoon at the planning department.

How would he explain his sudden arrival to Maggie? Hell, he couldn't even explain it to himself. He could call first and say he was worried about Elliott. Or he could say he'd forgotten some important papers he had to have. He turned around and headed back toward the phone booth he'd just left, but someone else was in it. He walked around the booth and looked at his watch. If he was going, he'd better get going. He felt a rush of relief. Everything he had to say could be better said in person than on the phone.

He crossed the street and walked back to his car smiling to himself. He was tired of imagining Maggie. He'd drive home tonight and surprise her and Elliott, and drive back tomorrow for the meeting. The solution was so simple he didn't know why he hadn't done it sooner.

At eleven he pulled up in front of a dark house. When he reached for the front-door key behind the ivy in the flower box, he found it wasn't there. He muttered a curse and tripped on one of Elliott's small racing cars. The key had been there for two years; Maggie had been there for a few weeks and the key disappeared.

He walked around under Maggie's window and stared up at it. After trying the kitchen window and the back door, he finally remembered that the front window behind the porch swing was never locked.

He smiled to himself in the dark as the window slid up at his touch. He was halfway through the open window when he felt the sharp crack of a plastic bat on the top of his skull. He fell forward to the floor from surprise and from shock. Looking up he saw a blurry Maggie standing over him in her T-shirt, an oversize, red plastic baseball bat in her hands.

"Why didn't you tell me?" she demanded, her eyes wide with fright.

He rubbed his head. "You didn't give me a chance," he protested.

"I mean before you came. You...you..." She kneeled down next to him. "I could have killed you."

She wasn't wearing anything under her T-shirt and he could see the outline of her breasts, the points where the nipples raised the fabric. His breath came in short gasps, rough and uneven.

"Are you all right?" she asked anxiously.

"I don't know." His voice was unsteady.

Maggie held out her hand to help him up, but when he took it he pulled her down on top of him. Her body resisted for a fleeting second, then softened and melted into his.

He'd been imagining how she would feel pressed next to him ever since the night they threw the ice in the pond, and now that it was real he didn't ever want to let her go. He put his arms around her waist, his hands moved to cup her firm bottom.

"What are you doing?" she murmured.

He shifted his body so that her hips rested on his and her lips were only a breath away. "I don't know, I'm delirious," he confessed, a slow smile spreading across his face. His hands cradled her face and her lips met his and merged and he felt himself drowning in their sweetness. Her heart throbbed through his body until it matched his own. His hands felt the edge of the T-shirt and her face swam in and out of his consciousness. Maybe it was a dream, after all.

"Garrett." Maggie pulled away from him by bracing her hands on the floor. "I've got to make sure that you're okay, that you don't have a concussion."

"Why don't you give me a thorough checkup?" he suggested with a wicked gleam in his eye.

Maggie blushed and sat on the floor next to him. She hugged her body to keep from shaking. She thought it was because of the fright of seeing Garrett come through the window, but deep down she knew it was more than that. She put her hand on his forehead and he winced.

"Where does it hurt?" she asked anxiously.

He reached for her hand and guided it to a bump on the back of his head. He moaned softly as her fingers moved from the base of his neck to the top of his head.

"Oh, Garrett, I'm sorry. Let me get some ice for it."

"No, don't leave."

"But I'm afraid—"

"So am I. I'm afraid you'll leave." He took her hands and laced his fingers through hers.

"You *must* be delirious." Maggie leaned forward to study his tanned face and his dark brown eyes which held her there. She felt the border between nanny and woman begin to waver and fade with every passing moment. When she saw his jaw tighten and his eyes darken with undisguised passion, her heart pounded more furiously.

"I'm delirious over you," he whispered. He propped himself up on one elbow and ran his finger over her lips. "You're trembling," he said, and kissed her gently on the lips.

Maggie fought for control over her body and her brain. He was talking nonsense, the first sign of a concussion. There was a procedure—ask questions, check the eyes.

"Garrett." Her voice was urgent. "Count to one hundred for me."

He grinned. "Whatever you say. Ten, twenty, forty..." He pulled her to him and covered her lips with his until she felt herself melting under the pressure. If this was a concussion she must have one, too. If he was out of his mind she was further out of hers for letting this happen. Whatever it was, they were in this together.

Chapter Five

Somewhere in the back of her mind Maggie was conscious of noise and movement. She pulled herself out of Garrett's arms and stood up on shaky legs. "Elliott," she whispered, her eyes wide with fear. She spun on her heels and ran up the stairs, leaving an astonished Garrett on the floor. What on earth was she thinking of, lying in the arms of her employer on the floor of his living room while his son slept upstairs? Or worse, didn't sleep upstairs. What if Elliott had found them there like that?

At the top of the landing Maggie stopped abruptly. Elliott was coming out of the bathroom with his eyes half closed. When he rounded the corner on his way back to his room, Maggie followed softly and stood in the doorway while he climbed into his bed and instantly fell asleep.

With a sigh of relief Maggie slipped back into her own room. If Garrett had enough strength to pull her into his arms and kiss her the way he did, then he had enough strength to get himself to bed. She felt terrible about hitting him over the head but even worse about allowing the situation to deteriorate into a free-for-all after that.

She heard footsteps on the stairs and she stiffened and lay rigid on her bed. Garrett walked past her room to Elliott's and opened his door. She could picture him standing there in the doorway just as she had done watching Elliott sleep. Maybe he hadn't heard anything. Maybe he didn't believe that Elliott had ever been awake at all. She could feel the uncertainty in the air.

Maggie pulled the sheet over her head. Coward, she whispered to herself. She could not speak to Garrett or even see him again tonight. Her lips still tingled from his kiss and her whole body shook at the memory of her body on top of his. Finally after an eternity of waiting, she heard him close Elliott's door and go downstairs.

Maggie approached the kitchen cautiously the next morning, but the only person there was Elliott eating cereal at the table.

"My dad's home," he announced importantly, a small smile on his face that was so like Garrett's her heart gave a lurch.

"Really?" She looked out the front window where his car was parked in the driveway.

"How do you know?" she asked carefully. "Did you see his car?"

"I saw him. Could I have some toast?"

Maggie reached for the bread. "Where?"

"Here." Elliott pointed to the kitchen floor. "But he went back to bed. He said to tell you he has a headache."

Maggie nodded. I'll bet he does. She looked at the school lunch menu taped on the wall. "Are you having hot lunch today, Elliott? It's pork cutlet and mashed potatoes."

Elliott answered by wrinkling his nose and opening his mouth to make a gagging sound. Maggie automatically reached for a brown paper bag and filled it with things he liked—crackers, carrot sticks, salami and cheese.

She walked Elliott to the bus stop at the end of the road. "I wonder why your dad came home," she asked casually. "Did he say?"

Elliott finished chewing the piece of toast in his mouth and looked at Maggie. "I think he forgot something."

The school bus left a cloud of dust behind it and Maggie dragged the heels of her old running shoes as she walked slowly back to the house. Sooner or later she would have to face Garrett and tell him what he already knew. They couldn't carry on like that any more.

He was standing on the front porch with a cup of coffee in his hand, watching her as she approached. His eyes were heavy with sleep and there was no visible bump on his head. She fought off a desire to run her fingers through his hair to look for one. She had the feeling that if she quickened her step just a fraction he'd open his arms and she'd fall right into them. And they'd be right back where they left off last night, only this time the house was empty. There would be no interruptions.

Maggie took a deep breath of the cool, fresh morning air to give her strength. The sleepy, satisfied smile on Garrett's face told her she was going to need it. It was time to go on the offensive, and when she finished he might not be smiling any more.

"Garrett—"

"Looks like it's going to be a beautiful day. Too bad I can't stick around."

"Garrett, about last night—"

He shrugged and stretched his arms toward the sky, his blue T-shirt taut over his broad chest. "Don't apologize, Maggie, it's partly my fault."

"Partly?" She stepped forward and stared at him wide-eyed, but he put his hand on her shoulder.

"Yes, I should have told you I was coming back. You were just doing your job."

"I know that." She put her hand on his to take it off her shoulder, but he misunderstood and pulled her to him and kissed her, slowly and gently, savoring the moment. He tasted like coffee and Maggie smelled sunshine on the wet grass all around them.

Garrett's kiss deepened, and Maggie knew she should object. Yet she did nothing about it. Except to put her arms around his neck and feel tremors moving from her scalp to her toes. She wiggled her toes inside the running shoes and finally the voice in her head that was clamoring to be heard got through to her befuddled brain and she pulled away.

"Garrett," she gasped, "I gave you the wrong impression last night."

He shook his head. "The only impression I got was that you were protecting my house and my child. It isn't your fault that my head got in the way." He reached up and ran his hand through his hair and she remembered how thick it felt to her fingers last night.

"How is your head?" she asked.

"Better." He sat down on the porch step and looked up at her, his eyes traveling slowly over her bare legs, her long shirt that almost covered her shorts.

She shifted from one foot to the other. She didn't like looking down at him, but she didn't want to sit next to him on the step, either. She'd better say what she had to say and go back into the house.

"What I'm talking about is what happened after I hit you on the head."

He rubbed his forehead. "Oh, yes, I wanted to ask you about that."

Suddenly Maggie's knees were so weak she had to sit down. She chose the step next to the railing, as far from him as possible.

"We have to take precautions to make sure it doesn't happen again," she said sternly.

"Oh, we will," Garrett assured her, moving to the top step to give her an earnest look. "I'm going to put that key back where it belongs. Where is it, anyway?"

"I hid it on top of the light fixture on the porch. The flower box was too obvious. That's the first place somebody would look."

"Maggie, this is the country. Nobody's going to break into our house. We keep the key in an obvious place so we can find it when we need it. Like last night."

"Oh. Well, I'm not talking about that, anyway."

He drew his eyebrows together in a puzzled frown. "What else do you want me to do? I know, I'll call first. No more surprises. How's that?"

"Fine, but—"

"I'm grateful to you, Maggie, for everything."

His eyes crinkled at the edges and a corner of his mouth turned up in a knowing grin. Maggie blushed. It was bad enough to have broken every rule in the nanny's code, but to be reminded of it was humiliating.

"Even though you knocked me out cold," he continued, "and gave me amnesia."

Maggie's eyes widened in disbelief. "You mean you don't remember what happened?"

"Not after you hit me," he assured her, touching her cheek with his finger. "Do you know how I got to bed?"

She shook her head, his touch making her cheek flame.

"I must have been on automatic pilot." He stood up and reached for her hand to pull her up with him.

"What did you come home for anyway?"

"I forgot something, something I needed." He looked at her hair and her eyes, then his gaze lingered on her mouth.

"Did you find it?" she asked breathlessly.

"Yes, it was right where I left it." They exchanged a long look on the top step of the porch as the sun's rays reached the slanting roof. All of Maggie's protests, all her good intentions seemed stuck in her throat. Garrett flashed her a brief smile before he disappeared into the house.

Maggie leaned against the railing for support. How was it possible that a man she'd never seen until a few weeks ago had the power to turn her into a dizzy, helpless, inarticulate...

Just as suddenly as he disappeared, Garrett reappeared on the porch in a striped, button-down shirt, frayed at the cuffs but clean, with a briefcase in his hand. "I'm late," he explained.

"Have you had breakfast?" she asked automatically.

He shook his head. "I'll take a rain check on that." He paused in front of his car. "And on anything else I missed out on."

Maggie sat on the porch for a long time trying to sort out her feelings. First there was a sense of relief that he had finally left, which was sometimes hard to separate from regret and disappointment.

She dragged herself into the house and washed the breakfast dishes. Although she often found a release for tension in housework, this was not one of those times. She went out the back door and walked slowly around the fish pond, stopping occasionally to look in the water at her reflection.

The sensible nanny she expected to see there did not materialize. The face that looked back at her had a crooked smile, the cheeks were flushed and lips were full and looked as if they'd been kissed. She shook her head in disgust. "Shape up," she told the face in the water, "or ship out."

When Garrett's call came that evening, Maggie was prepared. She'd reread the *Nanny's Handbook of Etiquette* and an introductory book to psychology, which was required reading for all students. She had Garrett figured out and she knew what to do about him.

She was ready, but so was he. "I've made a decision," he announced.

"So have I," she countered.

"I want you to stay."

"I have to leave."

"No, you don't. I called Mrs. Newcastle."

"Well, you can call her back. My being here is a big mistake. I should have left the day I came. I'm not the right person for this job. You said so yourself."

"That was then. We're talking about now. I'll admit you made some mistakes at the beginning, like telling Elliott that

Mary Poppins lived with dinosaurs, and even recently like changing the hiding place of the front-door key. But I can overlook that. You're a quick learner and I have high hopes for you."

Maggie kicked her stockinged foot against the refrigerator in frustration. "I appreciate that, Garrett, but unfortunately I have no hopes for you, at all. You promised me there'd be no more..." she hesitated. "Physical contact," she said lamely, "and yet this morning—"

"I kissed you. You're right, as usual. But you looked so fresh and delicious, like a ripe peach, and you smell like summer flowers and you feel like—"

Maggie reached for a kitchen chair and sat down with a thud. "Garrett, you shouldn't be saying these things."

"I know. I should wait until I see you."

"You can't say them at all, anywhere. I said physical contact, but I meant verbal contact, too. It's not your fault entirely. I realize that I may have acted in an improper manner not befitting a nanny."

"Don't worry," he assured her. "I didn't mention it to Mrs. Newcastle and I never will. Not even if she tortures me. Now that we've settled that..."

Maggie sighed. What had been settled? she wondered. "The only reason I would consider staying is for Elliott."

"That's the only reason I want you to stay. Elliott likes you and he's happy. And when Elliott's happy, I'm happy. And we'll try to make you happy, too."

Maggie closed her eyes and rested her forehead on the table. Garrett had a way of turning everything she said around.

After Maggie put Elliott on the school bus the next day she walked across the fields that she could see from the house. Hay was stacked in neat bundles and there was the hum of a tractor in the distance. In a few weeks it would be Halloween and she would still be with Garrett and Elliott, and then Thanksgiving and where would she be? In spite of her fears and protests there was a warm feeling around her heart when she thought about Garrett asking her to stay on.

She paused and looked back at the old farmhouse, its slanted roof outlined against the hazy autumn sky. There was a feeling of home about the place that Maggie felt drawn to. If she was to stay there she must learn to keep Garrett at arm's length. She was only too aware that Garrett had never forced himself on her. She could have pushed him away, she could have said no, but she didn't.

Why not? She ran through the fields and arrived breathless at the house. She put some of Elliott's cereal in a bowl and poured milk over it. Faces of missing children stared back at her from the milk carton. Why didn't Elliott's mother ever call him or write to him or want to see him?

Maggie was determined to ask Garrett about his ex-wife, but that night on the phone he was so eager to tell her about his plans for the weekend she didn't want to spoil his excitement.

"I'll be down Friday night to pick you up," he told her.

"Me? You mean Elliott."

"You, too. I need you. I have the surveyor coming on Saturday, and we have to mark off the boundary lines. And I want you to see it now before I decide whether to make an offer on it, whether it's worth what they're asking."

Maggie was determined not to go. The land represented his new life when she would be gone, and she didn't want to think about it. "What about my day off?" she asked.

"Take Monday off or Tuesday. I'm flexible, why can't you be? This may be the last weekend before the rain. It's still Indian summer up here, it's beautiful."

It was beautiful with the fields of sun-bleached grasses, the soft, dry air, the river that gurgled instead of rushing past as it did when it was swollen with rain. So beautiful that Garrett was seized with an urgent sense that Maggie must see it with him. He leaned against the glass wall of the phone booth and waited for her answer. What if she didn't like it, at all? What if she couldn't imagine green lawns where there were now overgrown weeds? What if she hated sleeping on the ground in a tent and cooking over a camp fire? Lots of women did. But Maggie wasn't lots of women. She was . . . she was only his son's nanny. How many times did he have to remind himself?

Still he gripped the receiver tightly and waited for her answer.

"I am flexible," she insisted, "but—"

"Good. The first thing is to get the tents out of the back closet and air them out. The sleeping bags are there, too."

"I don't have a sleeping bag."

"I have one for you."

"And a tent?"

"Everything."

He heard her sigh and he smiled to himself.

When Garrett arrived Friday night the sleeping bags were hanging over the porch railing and the tent was leaning against the shed. Brown bags full of groceries stood on the kitchen table. Elliott ran to meet his father before he'd gotten out of the car.

"We're having hot chocolate and popcorn and gingerbread with lemon sauce and—"

"Wait a minute," Garrett said as they walked toward the house where Maggie stood looking down at them. "We only have a camp fire to cook over."

He stood smiling up at Maggie while she wiped her hands against her large white apron. Her hair was tousled and there was a white smudge of flour on her nose. He took the steps two at a time and brushed the flour off with his fingers. Her lips were so close to his that he would have kissed her if Elliott hadn't been there. He was losing control of the situation, he realized, and the weekend had only begun. Maggie took a step backward and he put the brakes on his emotions.

"You can do a lot with a Dutch oven," she explained, shooting warning glances at him.

"I thought you'd never been camping," he said, smiling innocently.

"I haven't, but I took a class in outdoor cooking. I was a nutrition major."

Garrett shook his head. "You amaze me, Maggie. You are the perfect nanny. Remind me to give you a raise." He rested his hand on the top of her shiny hair, intending to pat her head, but lingering too long.

Elliott ran out to the car with a bag of groceries and Maggie ducked under Garrett's hand. "There's only one tent," she said suspiciously.

Garrett raised his hands, palms up. "It's yours. Elliott and I will sleep under the stars."

"That sounds nice," she said, mollified.

"It is nice. Okay, you have the stars, I'll take the tent."

Elliott was back for another load. "I want to sleep in the tent," he said.

"That's all right," Garrett told him. "Because Maggie and I want to sleep outside." He grinned at her. Keep it light, he told himself, it's the only way.

Maggie cleared her throat and glared at Garrett.

Maggie was quiet on the ride to the Stanislaus River property. She stared straight ahead of her on the long, winding highway that stretched up into the foothills of the Sierras. Garrett watched her face carefully as he pulled into the clearing in the middle of the twenty acres. Elliott ran down to the river's edge.

"What do you think of an underground house?" Garrett asked, pointing to a slope that faced the river.

"It sounds dark and dank," she answered quickly.

Garrett took her arm and pulled her to the slope. "It won't be dark or dank because it will have a glass wall facing southwest." He pointed toward the river, hoping to shake her out of her mood. "And a skylight."

"Skylights leak." She pulled her arm away from him.

"It will be made like shingles, so that the one above laps over the one below." He could see it so clearly there nestled in the hill. Why couldn't she see it, too?

"What if the house collapses under the weight of the earth?" Maggie persisted.

"We'll wear helmets. No, I'm kidding. The roof will be reinforced, and the support beams are designed for over-stress." He folded his arms across his chest and moved to block her view of the river so she would have to look at him. "What's wrong?"

She shook her head. "Nothing." Her chin was set at a defiant angle, and he couldn't understand what had set her off. "Can I ask you a question?"

"Of course."

"Why doesn't Elliott's mother ever call him or come to see him?"

His face felt stiff. Anger at Helena made his chest feel tight. He looked around to make sure Elliott was still down at the river's edge.

"She's not interested in seeing him. Isn't that apparent?"

Maggie saw the lines deepen in Garrett's forehead. She knew he didn't like talking about Helena, but she had to ask, had to know what happened.

"I thought maybe she didn't know where he was," she suggested.

"She knows. I didn't just walk out with him and leave no forwarding address." He paused. "Is that what you thought?"

Maggie took a deep breath. "No...I didn't know. I couldn't believe she'd just let him go. If he were my son..." Tears sprang to Maggie's eyes. Why was it that people who didn't deserve children had them so easily, when women like her who wanted them so desperately couldn't have any?

Garrett put his hands on her shoulders and then reached up to wipe away a single tear that ran down her cheek. Maggie trembled.

"I know," he said softly. "You'd never let him go. But Helena is not like you, at all. She loves the wide, open sea and the thrill of the chase. She resents anything or anyone who keeps her from it. I'm not saying she doesn't have re-grets. She's not a monster, but she has to live with her decision. When push came to shove she had to make a choice, and freedom and money and excitement won out.''

Maggie gulped. "And Elliott lost."

Garrett nodded. "Try explaining that to a four-year-old."

Maggie looked at him inquiringly and he shook his head. "I didn't do a very good job of it. I didn't want him to know that his mother didn't want him, so I grabbed him and we took off. Without his things, as you noticed, but with Helena's approval."

Garrett's eyes were dark with the pain of remembering and Maggie longed to reassure him he'd done a great job with Elliott and that she understood.

Elliott came running up the bank to join them and Maggie hugged him tightly. Careful, she told herself. Don't try to make it up to him all at once. Go slowly. She changed into her swimming suit behind a bush while Garrett went back to the car for huge, rubber inner tubes so they could float down the river.

The water was low, but still deep and swift enough to carry them downstream. Maggie felt her bottom scrape the mud as she pushed off from the gently sloping bank. Garrett grabbed her by the hand and Elliott by the other and they floated slowly past bushes and brambles and the trees on Garrett's property. The sky was hazy and the soft air caressed Maggie's face and shoulders. Elliott shrieked with delight at every wave that splashed his face, and Maggie caught Garrett's eye and smiled.

The cool water flowed past her taking her worries with it. She leaned her head back against the black rubber tire and let the sun shine on her face. She tried to remember if she had ever been so happy and she couldn't.

They finally pulled themselves out of the water and walked back to their campsite in the middle of the clearing. Maggie unloaded her picnic basket and set out meat and cheese and bread, lettuce and tomato. Garrett looked over the food and sent Elliott to gather firewood.

"We're just having sandwiches," Maggie told him.

"Grilled sandwiches," he corrected her, lighting a match to a piece of newspaper under a pile of sticks. He threw slices of cheese and salami in the frying pan, let them sizzle, then flipped them onto thick slices of French bread.

Maggie bit into a golden, toasted melted-cheese-and-salami sandwich and sighed with contentment. "I thought I was going to cook," she commented, too happy to protest.

"You always cook."

"I like to. It's my job. You're paying me for it. I was a—"

"I know, a nutrition major. But I've been eating out all week. And you've been cooking. It's my turn."

"I just want to be useful."

"You are useful, you're the most useful person I've ever met. And you're decorative, too." His eyes travelled over her black tank suit, still wet from the river.

Elliott chewed thoughtfully and his eyes traveled back and forth, following the conversation.

Maggie crossed her legs in front of her and ate with her plate balanced on her knees. After he finished his sandwich Elliott toasted marshmallows on sticks that he'd whittled to make sharp points at the ends. He carefully sandwiched each marshmallow between graham crackers with a square of chocolate and handed one to Maggie and one to Garrett.

Then he went down to the river to wash his hands, taking his fishing pole with him. "Come and fish with me when you're done," he told Maggie. She promised she would.

Maggie heated water for tea in an old, blackened pot and Garrett changed back into clothes behind the same bush she'd used. He had an appointment with the surveyor after lunch. His hair was still wet when he came back to the fire. Slicked back from his face it made his strong features stand out and she couldn't help staring at him. He stared back and Maggie heard the water boil, but she didn't take the pot off the fire. She didn't do anything but stand and look into Garrett's deep, dark eyes.

She was aware that her swimming suit clung to her body, very much aware that from the way Garrett was looking at her she might as well have been wearing nothing at all, and yet she made no effort to move. She just stood there feeling the heat from the flames and the heat from his gaze, and still she shivered.

When the water finally bubbled over and sputtered onto the fire, Maggie jerked her eyes away from Garrett and bent over to pick up the pot.

She grabbed a tea bag and stirred the water briskly. Much too briskly. "I'm going fishing this afternoon," she explained. "I hope we catch something for dinner."

"You will. I'm counting on you." Garrett's voice was low. "But first you'd better get the marshmallow off your lips." He moved around the smoldering fire to kiss her fiercely. Her tin cup fell out of her hands, the tea sloshed on the ground. Her lips clung to his, but Maggie couldn't blame it on the marshmallows.

"Garrett," she gasped. "What about the surveyor?"

He ran his hand down her back to where her spine curved in and his fingers lingered on the edge of her swimming suit. He looked at her flushed cheeks and soft lips. When he ran his tongue over her lower lip she thought she might faint.

"I think I got it all," he said, his voice rough against her ear. Then he gave her a brief smile and took off at a run down the path to the road. So he was late for his appointment, Maggie thought, staring off in the direction of the dust he kicked up.

She was disgusted with herself for allowing this situation to continue. Not only to continue but to get worse. She stamped out the embers with more force than she intended, then poured water on them. Elliott's voice reminded her that he was waiting for her. She pulled an oversized T-shirt over her swimming suit and went down to the river.

He already had several striped bass in his bucket and he wanted her to admire them. She baited her own hook and sat down on the bank next to him.

"What do you want to be when you grow up, Elliott? A fisherman like your dad?"

"My dad is a marine biologist," he corrected her, standing up to untangle his line.

"That's right, I forgot."

"My mom is a fisherman."

Maggie tensed and watched his face out of the corner of her eye. "Did you used to go fishing with her?" she asked, at last.

He nodded. "On her boat. We went fast so the Coast Guard wouldn't catch us."

"Why did they want to catch you?" Maggie watched the float bob up and down in the water.

"'Cause we took too much salmon," he explained.

"That must have been exciting." Maggie kept her voice even, carefully not approving or disapproving.

Elliott threw his line into the moving water. "I was scared they'd arrest us."

Maggie had a vision of a smaller, younger Elliott ripping through the water in a trawler hotly pursued by the law. It must have been a terrifying experience.

"I wasn't supposed to tell my dad," he said, pushing his glasses up his nose and frowning at the worm on the end of his hook.

"Did you?" she asked, holding her breath. Garrett had said nothing about Helena breaking the law.

He nodded. "He was mad, but he didn't tell on me."

Tears sprang to Maggie's eyes at the thought of a little boy caught in the middle, and she turned to look downstream so Elliott couldn't see her face.

They fished in silence until Maggie hauled in an eight-inch bass. Elliott smiled approvingly.

"What does decorative mean?" he asked suddenly.

"Decorative?" Maggie squinted into the afternoon sunlight reflected on the water. "Well, it means nice to look at. Your dad was just being polite when he said that."

Out of the corner of her eye she saw Elliott studying her profile.

"My dad doesn't say things to be polite."

Maggie had to admit to herself that this was true.

Back at the campsite with a full bucket of fish, Maggie and Elliott found Garrett talking to a man in overalls holding a telescope on a tripod. The man looked up and Garrett introduced them.

"This here's a nice piece of property, Mrs. Townsend."

"Oh, no, I'm not—"

"Looks like there's two more acres than we figured." He tapped his telescope.

"That's good news, but it's really not my—"

The surveyor shook his head and looked at Garrett. "Maybe she can't appreciate it now, but once you get it cleared and build your house, she'll come around."

"I tried to tell her about the earth-sheltered house," Garrett said without bothering to explain that Maggie was not Mrs. Townsend, "but she couldn't picture it."

The surveyor chuckled. "My wife wouldn't take to living underground, either."

"It will have a glass wall facing southwest," Maggie explained, "and a skylight."

"Well, well." The surveyor looked from Maggie to Garrett and then at the house site. "You don't say." Then he folded his tripod and waved goodbye.

"He thinks I'm your wife," Maggie noted after a brief silence.

"You didn't say you weren't." Garrett began scraping the scales off a fish.

"Neither did you," she countered, unpacking the ingredients for her gingerbread. She beat eggs in silence for several minutes.

Garrett glanced up. "What do you think of it?"

"Looks fine," Maggie said absently, setting her gingerbread into the Dutch oven on top of the stove.

"I mean the land."

She bit her lip to keep from blurting, I like it, I love it, I want to live here with you in an underground house with the sun streaming through the glass wall.

"It's nice," she said firmly, then smiled with relief when Elliott appeared, his arms filled with sticks to feed the fire.

After Garrett had finished frying the fish, Maggie sat cross-legged on a log in front of the fire and pulled out potatoes baked in the coals. She put one on each of their plates. She thought nothing had ever tasted as delicious as the fresh bass with a squeeze of lemon on it. She used another lemon to make a sauce for her gingerbread and served it hot.

Garrett leaned back against a tree and closed his eyes after the first bite. Maggie watched him anxiously. Did he like it?

Finally he opened his eyes and smiled a lazy smile that turned Maggie's limbs to mush. "I like it," he said. "It reminds me of something my mother used to make."

"Your mother?" Garrett had talked about his grandparents' house on the Columbia River, but he had never mentioned any parents.

"Is your mother still—"

"Baking gingerbread? No. She's recovering from a broken hip, and she doesn't bake anymore. We're going up to see her at Thanksgiving."

"And your father?"

"He died when I was in college. The insurance money put me through school. That and my summer jobs on the boat."

Having heard all this before, Elliott became restless. "Can't you put the tent up now, Dad?" he asked, standing behind his father with his hands on Garrett's shoulders.

Garrett stood up and stretched. He would have liked to have the tent and Maggie to himself tonight. She looked so desirable sitting there on the ground, her face smudged with ashes, her usually straight, shiny hair tucked behind her ears. He imagined what they would do if they were alone and Maggie weren't his son's nanny. A late-night skinny dip in the river and then two sleeping bags zipped together.

She stood up suddenly, as if she had read his thoughts. She put a pan of water on the fire to heat for dishwater. If they were alone and Maggie were not the nanny was only part of it. If she didn't have such high standards, if she weren't afraid of breaking the rules; in other words, if she weren't Maggie. But she was, and he found it harder and harder to stop thinking about her, about her long legs, her lips, her hair, her gentle hands. He hammered the final stake and stood back to look at the tent without really seeing it.

Elliott dragged his sleeping bag and foam pad into the tent and peered out the narrow opening. No need to ask Elliott to join him in a skinny dip; he was in for the night. Garrett laid Maggie's pad and sleeping bag next to Elliott's while she was washing the pans from dinner.

He didn't linger by the camp fire. Instead he plunged through the bushes and down to the river. He hoped the cool water would cool his passion, but it didn't. After his swim, Garrett flung his sleeping bag and an air mattress down a few feet away from the tent. From inside the blue-and-gray domed tent he could hear Maggie's voice.

"Once upon a time about two-hundred million years ago, the world was warm and wet like a tropical garden."

"Even here?" Elliott asked.

Garrett reached for his hooded sweatshirt in his duffel bag. Then he stretched out on his back and leaned his head against his rolled-up sleeping bag to listen to the story.

"Oh, yes, especially here. In fact, right down by the river there lived a plant-eating dinosaur named camptosaurus. One day he was lying on his back floating downstream."

Lying on his back in the darkness, Garrett smiled.

"Just like we did today," Elliott remarked.

Maggie continued with her story, and Garrett closed his eyes and let the sound of Maggie's voice wash over him. It had a hypnotic quality and was like a verbal massage.

When she finished, she told Elliott good-night.

"Good night, Maggie." Elliott raised his voice. "Good night, Dad."

Garrett got up and opened the front flap to the tent. There was space between Maggie and Elliott that was almost big enough for another person. No, it wasn't. What was the matter with him? It was a beautiful night, a little cool with a mist rising off the river, a few clouds racing across the moon but nothing threatening, a perfect night to sleep outside. But not alone.

"Good night, Elliott," he said, reaching in to zip up Elliott's sleeping bag and kiss him on the cheek. Maggie was sitting up, looking at him, and he kissed her, too, quickly before she could turn away and disappear into her sleeping bag. He heard her sharp intake of breath and he smiled at her.

Reluctantly he left the tent and went to find a flat place in the clearing to sleep. He lay on his back watching the stars and thinking about his house with the glass wall and the earth roof. He wondered if Maggie could picture herself living here.

He didn't think so. Oh, yes, she cooked outside, she fished and she floated downstream in his river. But she was a nanny, as she kept reminding him, a graduate nanny with honors. A nanny doing her job and doing a damn good job of it, too, he admitted. If she weren't so good at it, he might have suspected she was doing it because she loved the land and loved Elliott and maybe she felt something for him, too.

Maggie wants a baby, he reminded himself, not a six-year-old boy. And you, he reminded himself, already have what you want. He looked around at the hill where he planned to put his house, at the tall weeds that covered the hill and he slapped at a mosquito. A bright light in the sky that he had been watching disappeared over the horizon and he watched for it to reappear. If it did, it must be a satellite.

He wondered if Maggie had ever seen a satellite. He stared at the tent and heard a rustling inside of nylon against the inflatable mattress. He pulled his legs out of his sleeping bag and walked over and stood outside the tent.

"Maggie," he whispered.

Her head appeared at the opening, her eyes wide with surprise.

"I thought you were asleep," she whispered.

"I can't sleep. Do you want to see a satellite?"

She nodded. Just like that. He couldn't get over it.

"Get your sleeping bag. It's cool out here."

She didn't ask questions, she just followed him to the level rise he'd chosen to sleep on.

They lay flat on their backs next to each other, not touching, just staring up at the sky. Maggie shivered and Garrett clenched his fists and refrained from gathering her into his arms.

"Cold?" he asked.

"No."

He pictured their sleeping bags zipped together. It would take a few minutes and they'd be together, warm, only a heartbeat apart.

Her soft voice broke the silence. "Garrett," she said, "I appreciate your behavior this weekend."

"My what?" His voice was so gruff it surprised him.

"Your restraint. Mrs. Newcastle impressed on us how important it is to maintain the barriers between employer and employee, even under unusual circumstances like these." She waved her hand in the direction of the tent.

"Do you mean that there are some men who would take advantage of a nanny under these circumstances?" he asked, his voice heavy with desire.

He felt Maggie's eyes search his face, and he turned the corners of his mouth down to show his disapproval of such men.

"You can count on me to remember our agreement," he assured her.

Maggie nodded and looked back at the sky. "And I'm sorry I sounded critical about your underground house. I didn't know what I was talking about. I'll bet it will be warm and bright and sunny and...and...happy." Maggie's voice caught and she slid out of her sleeping bag and stood up before he could stop her.

"Wait a minute. You haven't seen the satellite," he said, startled by her sudden change of mood.

She brushed the back of her hand across her eyes. "I'm too tired. I'll see you in the morning."

Garrett watched clouds blot out the stars above him and thought about his cloudy relationship with Maggie. What had he said to make her leave so suddenly? He didn't need anything else to dampen his spirits, but the rain came anyway, lightly at first, then hard enough to penetrate his sleeping bag. He swore softly and thought of the vacant space between Maggie and Elliott in the tent.

The warm, dry cozy tent. He stood up, shook the drops on his sleeping bag and ran across the clearing.

Maggie and Elliott were both asleep and he carefully wedged his narrow air mattress between them and put his sleeping bag on top. The plastic mattress squeaked as he lowered himself onto it and he held his breath. Elliott's face was buried in the pillow he had brought from his own bed at home.

Maggie sighed and turned over. Her face was so close to his that he could feel her warm breath on his face, smell the wood smoke in her hair and the freshness of the river on her skin.

The rain drummed on the slanted roof of the tent, and Garrett ached to put his arms around Maggie and hold her to him. He shifted his body so that he lay on his side facing her. He heard a long, low hiss from beneath him, and felt his hip sink closer to the ground. His air mattress had sprung a leak. A mosquito buzzed in his ear, and when he tried to slap it his elbow touched Maggie's shoulder. She opened her eyes and gasped.

"Garrett," she whispered, "what are you doing in here? How could you do this, when you promised me." She sat up and hugged her sleeping bag to her, her eyes deep with misery. "You told me I could count on you."

Garrett sat up and grabbed her arm. "You can," he whispered as loudly as he dared, "but it's raining."

Maggie looked at the plastic lining above her, listened to the drops falling. "Oh." She stared at him for a long moment, her breasts rising and falling under her soft T-shirt. His fingers were still tight around her arm. "How long have you been in here?"

"Just long enough to puncture my air mattress." Garrett felt the remaining air ooze out with a prolonged hiss.

"What are you going to do now?" Maggie asked, a line forming between her eyebrows.

"I'm going to go to sleep," he said. And to prove his sincerity, he turned his back to her and faced Elliott. Unfortunately he couldn't blot out her image, even with his eyes squeezed shut. Every movement, every sigh made him want to turn around to look at her. To see for himself if her eyelashes made shadows on her cheeks when her eyes were closed, or if her forehead was smooth and untroubled when she slept. If she slept. Unable to resist any longer, he turned to look at her.

As Garrett turned, Maggie closed her eyes quickly. Garrett's presence in the tent had raised the temperature about ten degrees. She wanted to unzip her sleeping bag, but if she did, Garrett would know she was awake and she didn't want to talk to him or even look at him.

She didn't want to see his hair fall across his forehead, because she felt an unreasonable urge to push it back with her fingers. She didn't want to see his lips because she knew how they felt when he kissed her. Even now his lips were close enough to do it. She felt her face flush and she reached for her zipper, keeping her eyes shut.

"Maggie." Garrett's breath was warm in her ear.

She didn't move. She held perfectly still until she felt his eyes on her, his dark, penetrating eyes that had the power to force her to look at him whether she wanted to or not.

Reluctantly she opened her eyes and saw his face above her, his elbow resting on the deflated air mattress.

"Yes."

"I was listening to your story out there."

She closed her eyes. "Do you still object to having Mary Poppins interacting with dinosaurs?"

"It isn't historically accurate." His gaze drifted to her open sleeping bag and lingered on her long, loose T-shirt. "But she must have been quite a remarkable woman," he admitted.

Maggie pulled the edge of her sleeping bag up to her chin, despite the warmth radiating from her body. "I think so."

Garrett lay on his back and looked at the rain sliding down the roof of the tent. "What happened in the end?" he asked.

"You heard. Mary Poppins saves the day."

"I mean what happens to Mary Poppins after she spreads sunshine everywhere?"

"She doesn't spread sunshine." Maggie propped herself on her elbow and looked earnestly into Garrett's eyes. "I see Mary Poppins as a modern woman, more of a problem-solver."

"Okay. What happens to her after she solves everybody's problems?"

"In the book she waits until the wind changes, and on the first day of spring she floats off in the sky, just the way she came."

"Leaving her family behind, just like that."

"It wasn't her family. She had a job to do and she did it. As a nanny, it's important to know when to leave."

"No nanny would leave before Halloween, would she?" Garrett sat up and opened a flap so fresh air could come into the tent. The rain was only a light sprinkle now and the breeze might cool the fever that raged in him whenever Maggie was so close he could feel her breath against his cheek. "Halloween is Elliott's favorite holiday."

Maggie smiled. "Mine, too. I said I'd stay until you have a replacement for me, Garrett, so of course I'll be here for Halloween."

It was so easy to fall into the trap of feeling like one of the family, Maggie thought. Especially lying in a tent with the two of them, so close yet so far apart. Garrett was right to remind her that she was just a nanny and would be leaving one day.

The rain lowered the temperature, and the next day it was too cool to go swimming in the river. Garrett went into town to talk to the well-digger and then they drove home. As if on cue, Elliott talked nonstop about the coming holiday.

"I want to be a Ninja," he informed Maggie. "Can you make me a Ninja costume? I'll show you a picture of how they look. What are you going to be, Maggie? Parents dress up, too."

Parents. One hundred and seventy-five parents at the party and one nanny. She'd stand out like a sore thumb. "I don't know. Maybe I'll be a witch."

Garrett frowned. "You're not the type."

"How do you know?"

"I've observed you at close range."

Maggie blushed, thinking of sleeping next to him last night. She was sure she'd fallen asleep before he did. And she wondered if he'd slept at all without an air mattress. When she woke up he was up and dressed, cooking bacon and making oatmeal over the fire.

When she tried to protest his taking over her job again, he silenced her with a look. She noticed the lines that forked out around his eyes. Maybe he'd lain there all night waiting for daylight so he could cook breakfast. The oatmeal was smooth and creamy and sprinkled with raisins and the bacon was crisp and delicious.

"What type am I, then?" she challenged.

He took his eyes away from the road to look her over.

"Cinderella before she goes to the ball."

Maggie laughed. She felt gritty and grimy, disheveled and badly in need of a bath and clean clothes. "Wait till you see me after my fairy godmother gets a hold of me," she promised.

"Who's your fairy godmother? Mrs. Newcastle?"

"She must be, she sent me to you."

"I must remember to thank her for that."

"She'll be coming to make her home visit one of these days."

He frowned. "To inspect our home?"

"And you."

"Uh-oh."

Maggie smiled. It was too soon to worry about Mrs. Newcastle's visit in December when she needed a Halloween costume in two weeks.

Chapter Six

As it turned out, Maggie didn't have to worry about what to be for Halloween. Elliott's teacher called her and asked her to be the fortune-teller at the school party. The school would charge twenty-five cents a fortune and the money would be used to buy playground equipment. Maggie made Elliott's white Ninja costume first with a black belt and headband. Then she started on the fortune-teller's gauzy blouse, wide cummerbund and headband.

She bought a long, blond wig at a costume shop and a gold glittery mask to cover her eyes.

On the weekends when Garrett came home she interrupted her sewing to work with him collecting money and weighing fish. He was preoccupied with his work on the river property and even when he was home he spent hours on the phone with the contractor discussing the excavation and the clearing. He seemed to have no trouble remembering their agreement. She couldn't have asked for more correct behavior from an employer.

She was glad, very glad. She didn't once have to remind him of her position and of his. He had another set of keys made, put them on his key chain and never forgot them when he came home unexpectedly. In fact he never came home unexpectedly at all, until one Friday morning when he burst into the house and found Maggie at the kitchen counter surrounded by baskets and bags of bright round orange fruit. Behind her against the wall canning jars filled with pale orange and yellow fruit lined the open shelves.

Garrett stopped in the doorway and stared at the scene. The picture of Maggie surrounded by ripe, voluptuous fruit was one he wanted to savor. He came home to tell her he'd put a bid on the property, a low bid, but a bid. He wanted to see what she'd say, but now that he was there in the room with her, he couldn't tell her. He couldn't tell her because he couldn't speak.

With her glowing cheeks, her hair gleaming in the light from the kitchen ceiling, up to her elbows in round, golden fruit, she looked like the goddess of fertility. All he could do was stare at her.

Finally he found his voice. "What are those?" he asked, catching his breath from racing up the front steps and into the house. He forced his gaze from Maggie to the fruit.

"Persimmons," she answered. "We didn't expect you back until tomorrow." She looked at the calendar on the wall behind him.

"What are you doing to them? Where did you get them?" He heard himself talking too fast, afraid to tell her he'd made a commitment, afraid to ask her what she thought. He tore his eyes away from her face and looked at the full, glistening jars on the shelves behind her.

"One of your neighbors left them on the porch this morning. He had a bumper crop. He said it's been a good year for persimmons. So I'm making jam and chutney and whatever else I can think of."

Garrett crossed the kitchen and lifted a firm, round tip-pointed fruit from the counter. He had to do something. He couldn't just stand there looking at Maggie and all that ripe fruit anymore. His blood raced. It was fall and Maggie and nature's bounty got all mixed up in his mind. He wanted to taste, to savor, to plunder. But only persimmons, he told himself, and bit into it while Maggie watched. Then he felt his lips pucker and he made a strangling sound.

"Uh-oh, that must be the kind you're not supposed to eat until it's a little softer." Maggie's smile turned into a sympathetic grimace as his face went through contortions. She reached for a spoon and dipped into a large, bubbling pot on the stove. "Here, try this." She lifted a spoonful of jam to his lips and her hand grazed his cheek.

Fire leapt from her touch to his face and the tart-sweet taste invaded his mouth.

"How's that?" she asked.

Garrett backed into the kitchen table and leaned against it. "Fine, wonderful." How close had he come to throwing that spoon down and crushing her to him? The adrenaline still pumped through his body and he wondered how long he could continue to live like this. Or not live like this.

"What are you doing here today, Garrett?" she asked as if she'd felt nothing, knew nothing about what was going on.

He was proud of his casual tone when he answered. "I was just reading my tide table, and I realized that today is a minus-one low tide. And there I was on the river with no way to take advantage of it." He opened his arms. "So I came back to get you to help me gather mussels." There, that sounded believable.

Maggie took off her white apron, which was smeared with orange jelly and washed her hands in the kitchen sink. "What are mussels?"

"Mussels are delicious fruits of the sea. They're even better than persimmons."

Maggie followed him to the shed where he picked up two buckets and his toolbox.

"Mussels for dinner and whatever you want for lunch. We're eating at Duarte's. Nothing fancy, but I like it." He looked at Maggie sitting next to him in the truck, admiring the way her jeans fit snugly over her hips. He advised her to roll them up to the knees.

Garrett and Maggie weren't the only ones to take advantage of the low tide. Little children dotted the beach with their pant legs rolled up, leaning over, looking down into the tide pools.

Maggie looked down into the clear, green water to see starfish clinging to rocks and sea anemones swaying back and forth. A child picked up a tiny rock crab and shrieked when it tried to pinch her finger. Maggie looked at Garrett.

"Next time we'll bring Elliott," he promised, in answer to her unspoken question.

He took Maggie's hand and they jumped over pools and landed on rocks until they had left the children behind and had only seals for company. The sleek, silvery bodies of the sea lions lay on rocks in the sun, knowing that they were protected by a moat of water around them.

"How would you like to spend your days like that, Maggie, lying around in the sun without a care in the world, except to catch fish for your seal husband and teach your seal babies how to swim?"

Maggie's face froze and Garrett frowned. What had he said to take the joy out of her face?

"Normally the mussels are covered with water," he said as if nothing had happened, "but today they're ours for the taking."

"Will I like them?" Maggie asked, prying one black-shelled mussel from a rock.

He couldn't see her face, but her voice sounded normal and he breathed a sigh of relief. Whatever this sadness was that crept up on her, she was able to keep it under control.

"You'll love them after I submerge them in white wine and parsley and garlic and steam them."

"What about Elliott?"

"He eats them. He's a child of the sea."

Duarte's was almost empty that Friday afternoon. It was too late for lunch and too early for dinner for the regulars. Maggie ordered artichoke soup, made from artichokes out of the fields that could be seen from the restaurant windows.

It was too quiet. Maggie longed for some noise to escape into. She didn't want to think about the seals and their husbands and babies. She especially didn't want Garrett thinking about them. But she'd prefer that to his thinking about her.

"Are you sure that's all you want, Maggie, to be a nanny all your life?"

She opened a package of crackers and crumbled them into her soup. "Haven't we had this conversation before?"

"But I didn't know you then."

"Do you know me now?"

"Of course. I've eaten with you, slept with you . . ."

Maggie glared at Garrett and raised her eyebrows at the waitress behind the counter.

"I mean next to you, in the tent."

"I know what you mean."

"You even knocked me out. But I haven't made any impression on you, have I?"

Maggie sipped her soup slowly, unwilling to answer. If he only knew that just the sight of him caused her heart to pound madly in her chest, he wouldn't have to ask.

"What happened to Mary Poppins after she floated away?" he asked casually.

"She had some more adventures," she answered just as casually.

"She didn't get married and have children of her own?"

Maggie's heart sank. He hadn't changed the subject, after all. Maggie put her spoon down and gripped the edge of the table.

"Look, Garrett, being a nanny is a career, just like marine biology. It's not a stepping stone to something else. I've spent years getting ready for it and then a year at Mrs. Newcastle's for special training. This is my first job and I'm enjoying it tremendously." She smiled determinedly. "Thanks to you and Elliott for making me feel wanted. And when you don't need me anymore I'll find a new job and

there'll be new people and new problems for me to solve.''
She tried to smile again but it just wouldn't come. Instead
she felt like crying.

Garrett put his elbows on the table and spoke with his jaw
clenched. "Are you saying that Elliott and I are replaceable?"

"In a way. In the same way that I'm replaceable to you.
But you'll always be special to me, because you were my
first—" She bit her lip. "Do we have to talk about this now?
Isn't it remarkable enough that we've gotten this far? Can't
we just be grateful that we get along as well as we do, the
three of us, and not worry about the future?"

Brave words for somebody who worried about the future
every time Garrett touched her or looked at her. It took all
of Maggie's strength to say the words, all of her imagination to decide what the right words were. And still Garrett
didn't look convinced.

"Sure," he said and stood up to pay the bill.

Maggie went back to her persimmons that afternoon and
the house was filled with steam from her kettle and the
sweet/sour smell of the fruit. Garrett went out to the pond,
but he kept coming back to the kitchen, walking through to
get something or just passing by and looking in from the
outside.

At dinnertime Garrett edged Maggie out of the kitchen
and began scrubbing the mussels. She had to admit that the
broth smelled delicious, but she watched Garrett remove a
mussel from the shell with some anxiety.

"Close your eyes, Maggie," Garrett ordered, "and open
your mouth." The soft buttery mussel drenched in white
wine sauce was better than she'd imagined.

At the table Elliott launched into his favorite subject and
his favorite holiday.

"Don't forget to come home early next Friday, Dad," he
said. "The party starts at seven."

Garrett came home in plenty of time to find Elliott carving a pumpkin on the front steps and Maggie toasting

pumpkin seeds in the kitchen. Even though she was expecting him this time her pulse quickened when he appeared in the doorway, bigger and broader than she remembered and smelling like damp earth and fresh air. His clothes were rumpled and dirty and he held out his hands, palms up, in front of her.

"Don't touch me, Maggie, I've been examining a septic tank." He grinned. "You'll have to wait until I've had a shower." He paused at the bathroom door. "Do I have to wear a costume?"

Maggie shook her head. She'd spent the week finishing the white Ninja costume and her own outfit and had completely forgotten about Garrett.

When he came out of the shower he was wearing a soft, blue chambray shirt and his faded, well-worn jeans. He smelled like soap and Maggie had to fight off getting caught in the magnetic field that surrounded him.

She'd done so well this week, keeping busy, not thinking about him, not worrying about the future. But now that he was here, living, breathing and larger than life, she was acutely aware of his presence and the effect he had on her.

Maggie held the shopping bag that contained her long, blond wig and the rest of her costume on her lap on the way to Elliott's school. She was glad she'd been given something to do and a mask to hide behind. That way she wouldn't stand out as the only nanny in the room. And she wouldn't have to explain over and over that she wasn't Mrs. Townsend and she wasn't Elliott's mother.

The school cafeteria had been transformed into a giant haunted house with flickering green lights and kids screaming and running from table to table, bobbing for apples, puncturing balloons with darts and fishing with magnetic lines for prizes in a tub.

Elliott joined his friends, many of whom were also dressed like Ninjas. Maggie went to change in the girls' bathroom. She took off her T-shirt and put on a round-necked gypsy blouse. Then she peeled her jeans off and pulled a long red skirt on. She cinched her waist with the wide cummerbund and laced it up tightly.

When she saw that it forced her breasts halfway out of the blouse, she gasped in dismay at her reflection in the mirror. But by throwing the fringed shawl she'd brought over her shoulders, she was able to achieve some semblance of modesty.

She straightened her long, blond wig and tossed her curls so they fell over one shoulder. One beauty mark on her cheek completed the effect and she looked at herself once more in the mirror from behind her gold mask and congratulated herself on the transformation.

Back in the cafeteria she blinked rapidly behind the mask to get used to the semidarkness. Neither Garrett nor Elliott were anywhere to be seen, but even if they had been around Maggie was sure they wouldn't have recognized her. She didn't look at all like the sensible nanny they knew, and she didn't feel like her, either. Her stomach did a nervous flip-flop when she saw the line of customers waiting for her under the sign "Madame Grimaldi Sees All, Knows All, Tells All for Twenty-five Cents."

Maggie wondered exactly what "All" she was going to tell those people. But she sat down in front of the crystal ball and beckoned to the first person. Soon she heard herself predicting long lives, tall, dark strangers and ocean voyages for the adults and bright futures as astronauts and athletes for the children.

After an hour of nonstop talking Maggie stood and pushed back the curtain to see what was going on at the party and found herself staring straight into Garrett's eyes. No sign of recognition flickered across his face. His eyes took a tour of her gauzy blouse and Maggie smiled a seductive Madame Grimaldi smile at him and motioned for him to take a seat. She let her shawl fall away from her shoulders.

"Madame Grimaldi?" Garrett asked, raising one eyebrow inquiringly.

"Yes." Maggie's throat was so dry from having talked so much that the word came out as a croak.

Garrett's forehead wrinkled with concern. "Can I get you a drink?"

"Yes, please," she whispered, then sank into her chair, her shawl back in place.

When Garrett reappeared with a paper cup full of punch he eased his long body into the chair opposite her with the crystal ball between them. He set the cup and a quarter on the table and looked up expectantly. The laugh lines that fanned out from his dark eyes made him look faintly amused.

Maggie took a quick sip and cleared her throat. The sooner she got this over with the better.

"What questions do you have for Madame Grimaldi?" she asked in a deep, throaty voice that she hardly recognized. She bent over her crystal ball.

Her shawl dropped behind her chair and she felt Garrett's eyes on her breasts. She tried not to breathe, because every time she did she came farther out of the blouse.

"Do you read palms?" he asked, his voice sounding as breathless as if he'd just run a mile.

"Of course Madame Grimaldi reads palms," she said indignantly. "And tea leaves and whatever else she needs to predict the future. But it will cost an extra twenty-five cents. After all, the money will be used to buy a new swing set for the school. Madame Grimaldi keeps nothing for herself."

Garrett reached into his pocket. "You're all heart, Madame Grimaldi," he commented.

Maggie put her hand against her rapidly beating heart self-consciously.

Garrett laid his hand on the table. Maggie lifted the coin from his hand and frowned in concentration at the lines crisscrossing his palm. She touched his fingers gently, smoothing his rough skin. It was for a good cause, she reminded herself, not daring to look at him.

His fingers tightened around hers and a jolt of current hit her in the pit of her stomach. She looked up and his gaze held hers for a long moment. He knows, she thought, of course he knows. He's putting me on.

"What's wrong?" he asked finally, releasing her hand.

"Nothing," she answered quickly, looking down again. "Everything is fine. You have a very long life line here." She traced the crease.

"Long, yes, but will it be happy?"

"Very happy," she assured him.

She released his hand and he leaned back in his chair.

"What about children?" he asked.

Maggie spun her crystal ball around once and stared intently into its depths.

"I see a small boy with glasses."

"That's uncanny," he said admiringly. "Any more?"

"More?" Maggie's voice caught. "Yes, many more, a whole houseful."

"But I'm not married," Garrett told her.

"Really?" she asked in mock surprise. Then she held the ball up to the light from the ceiling. "You'll get married. I can see it clearly now."

Garrett leaned forward and looked at the other side of the ball.

"Who is it? What does she look like? Is it anyone I know?"

"She's a stranger, a beautiful stranger."

Garrett looked up at Maggie's wig. "Blond hair?"

Maggie's face flushed. "Yes." She rubbed an imaginary smudge from the crystal ball and looked pointedly at her watch. She was reaching her limits. "I think your time is up."

Garrett tilted his chair backward and pulled the curtain to one side. No one was waiting outside. He pushed his chair forward and put both hands on the table, only inches from hers.

"Just one more question."

She looked at his hands. "Go ahead."

"Can I take you home tonight?"

"No," she said quickly, taking her hands off the table and pressing them together in her lap.

"Why not? Are you married?"

"No, but I live with someone."

"Ohhh." He drew the word out slowly. "Lucky man. Is it something serious?"

She shrugged lightly. "I'm afraid you've used up your questions."

Garrett stood up. "Sorry, but you can't blame me for trying. You don't often meet someone who knows all the answers."

Garrett picked up her shawl from the floor and laid it over her bare shoulders, then with maddening slowness tied it just above her breasts. Maggie's skin burned where he touched it, and she tried to keep her body from shaking. All the confidence she'd felt hiding behind the mask was evaporating.

From the scarf, his hands moved to tilt her chin. "If your predictions don't come true, can I have my money back?"

A shock of hair had fallen over his forehead giving him the boyish look Maggie couldn't resist. His smile was teasing. With one hand he reached behind him and drew the curtain shut.

The smell of hot wax and fresh pumpkin filled the air and children's shrieks faded into the background as Garrett's hands moved around her waist and covered her wide sash. His fingers grazed the bottom of her breasts. Maggie leaned forward, afraid she might fall, and Garrett kissed her at last. Then she knew she was falling, falling into a hole so deep she might never get out, but for one moment, she didn't care. She leaned into the kiss and felt his hands caress her back and she wished he'd never stop until the liquid fire that raced through her veins consumed her completely. She put her hands on Garrett's chest and pulled back to catch her breath.

"I'm afraid you've got the wrong idea about gypsy fortune-tellers," she protested breathlessly.

Garrett struggled to keep his composure. He'd never felt Maggie respond like that and he was wildly, recklessly happy. "You mean you don't really have all the answers?"

"Not any more. I sold them all here tonight." Maggie jerked the curtain open and stepped outside. If she stayed another minute in that tiny room she'd lose the remnant of control she had left. With every minute that passed in that enclosed space with Garrett she felt her resistance melting faster than the candles inside the pumpkins. She edged carefully around him and joined the line to bob for apples.

Garrett stood staring after her and shaking his head. She lived in his house, washed his clothes and took care of his son, but tonight she was someone else, someone so desirable it required all of his willpower to resist her.

Elliott flung himself at Garrett's legs, his face and hands sticking to his pants.

"J.R. invited me to spend the night at his house."

Garrett put his hand on the top of Elliott's head. "Where is he? I'd better check this out with his parents."

Elliott grabbed Garrett's hand and pulled him across the room where J.R. was firing a water gun at a lighted candle.

His parents assured Garrett that they had invited Elliott and Garrett smiled his consent. That meant that he and Maggie would be alone in the house tonight. He must not think of her as a seductive fortune-teller, though. He must think of her as the woman who appeared at his house one day, stiff and starchy and proper. Because that was what she was going to turn into at the stroke of twelve. That was the real Maggie. And who was the real Garrett? he asked himself suddenly. The self-sufficient breeder of fish who had closed his heart two years ago, or the man who yearned for something he couldn't have?

He searched the crowded room with his eyes and finally he saw her, dressed in her jeans again and bobbing for apples. She looked up and smiled tentatively at him and Garrett's heart swelled with hope. He crossed the room in a few seconds and pulled her up by the elbows. "Let's get out of here," he said. "It's time to go home." He tried to keep the urgency and the desire out of his voice.

She looked around. "Where's Elliott?"

"He's spending the night with a friend." He couldn't keep the glee from showing in his face and she saw it.

"They invited him," Garrett explained. "That's all right, isn't it?"

"Of course. It's just that—"

"You don't trust me, do you?"

"I do, but..." Her voice dropped so low that he missed the end of the sentence. Had she really said, "But I don't trust myself"? Maybe he had imagined it because he wanted her to say it.

In the car he turned to Maggie. "Maybe you don't trust me because you heard I kissed the fortune-teller tonight."

Maggie smiled in the darkness. "She must have told you what you wanted to hear."

Garrett turned down the dirt road to the farmhouse, driving slowly to prolong the nearness of Maggie, knowing that once inside the house she'd turn into a nanny again.

"Did you get a chance to have your fortune told?" Garrett snapped his fingers. "I forgot. You already know what's in store for you. You've got your whole life planned."

"That's right," Maggie said, twisting her fingers in her lap. "Anyway, I heard that fortune-teller was a phony."

"Oh, no." Garrett swung into the driveway and turned off the engine. "Every bit of her was real, I can vouch for that. She knew exactly what she was doing. She said I'm going to have a long, happy life with a wife and lots of children. Funny how everyone thinks you have to be married to have a happy life. That's the part she didn't understand. Look at you, look at me, we're proof." Garrett turned to reach for Maggie's hand, but before he could touch her she'd opened the door and run up the steps and disappeared into the house.

He wasn't surprised to see her go. He was just surprised that it hurt so much, like a fist in the stomach. It was a good thing he hadn't asked her if she wanted to be a part of his long, happy life. He had no right to ask anyone that again. Not ever. He'd taken a chance once, married Helena, brought Elliott into the world and then his life had shattered into a million pieces.

Now that he had it back together again, he had to walk a straight line, run a tight ship…what else? His mind groped for another cliché, then ran out of excuses for falling for Maggie. If fate hadn't delivered her to his door, then he wouldn't have these problems, these sleepless nights. He wouldn't have Maggie. He groaned. He had to have Maggie.

Chapter Seven

Now that Halloween was safely behind her, Maggie found herself dreading the next holiday. It was the time of year when the whole world seemed to be paired up. Doreen had a new boyfriend she had met at the Monarch Butterfly Festival, the geese overhead flew south in pairs and the gray whales swam down the coast to Scammons Lagoon to mate and have their babies.

Yes, it was definitely a family time of year. A time of year that made Maggie more aware than ever that her life was not exactly what she had expected it to be. Despite all her brave words to Garrett about the rewarding life of a nanny, she had a hard time working up her enthusiasm for Mrs. Newcastle's annual Thanksgiving dinner for past and present nannies.

Even though she knew she wouldn't be cooking, she bought a ticket for the turkey raffle at Elliott's school and clipped recipes for stuffing from the food column of the newspaper.

You should be grateful, she told herself sternly. There were housewives all over the country who would love to trade places with her, who would like to sit down with civilized, sophisticated friends to a lovely catered dinner instead of sweating over a hot stove all day.

Maggie was punching down the dough for oatmeal bread when Elliott burst into the kitchen to tell her about their Thanksgiving trip to his grandmother's house in Oregon.

"If you win the turkey, you can bring it along," he told her, kneeling on a stool to watch her knead the bread.

"But Elliott, I'm not going to your grandmother's house," she said.

His blue eyes widened and he looked up at her in surprise. "Yes, you are. My dad said you were."

It was hard to contradict Garrett in this house, but Maggie knew she had to tell Elliott now before he made another scene like the one in the parking lot in Carmel when she hadn't agreed to go to the aquarium with them.

She turned the dough over and pounded it with her fists. How like Garrett to take her for granted, to assume that she'd go wherever they went without inviting her. Not that she would have gone. Being with someone else's family made an outsider feel even worse than ever. No, it was better to spend Thanksgiving with all the other nannies at Mrs. Newcastle's elegant town house in San Francisco.

Maggie looked up from the solid oak breadboard and took a deep breath. "Elliott, Thanksgiving is a time for families to get together. You're going to your grandmother's house to be with her, and I'm going to San Francisco to be with some friends."

He frowned. "Where's your family?"

"My family lives far away, all the way across the country, so I'm going to be with a big group of nannies just like me who don't have any...who don't have...who aren't able to be with their own families." Maggie struggled to present a picture of an upbeat event instead of a dreary dinner.

Elliott's lower lip jutted out in a stubborn way that reminded Maggie of Garrett.

"Will there be any kids there?"

"No, no kids. But it will be a real Thanksgiving dinner, even though Mrs. Newcastle is English and English people don't normally have Thanksgiving."

"What do they have?"

"Well, they have Boxing Day and Whitsun's Day and, oh, I don't know. You can ask her when she comes to see me next month. She'll want to meet you to see if I'm doing a good job with you."

He looked dubious. "I'll ask her if she knows how to make turkey and stuffing and pumpkin pie."

"I'm sure she does," she assured him. "She probably makes it just like your grandma does." Maggie didn't mention that the whole dinner would be catered.

"My grandma doesn't make it." Elliott hopped off the stool, went to the cookie jar and reached into it for a gingersnap.

Maggie covered the dough with a clean cloth and set it in the pantry to rise. "Is it because she's still recovering from her hip operation?" Maggie pictured a little, old gray-haired lady in a cozy cottage with an afghan over her lap.

"It's because she doesn't cook. She takes us to a restaurant or she buys it already made."

Maggie paused at the pantry door.

"So if you came, Maggie, and brought the turkey, you could cook it for her."

Maggie hung her apron on a hook and sat down at the table.

"Wait a minute, I haven't won the turkey yet. And another thing, maybe your grandma wouldn't want me to cook it. She doesn't even know me. Maybe she likes eating out."

Elliott shook his head. "She always says there's nothing like a home-cooked meal cooked by somebody else. Besides, she's tired when she comes home from work."

"Work?" Maggie's picture of Elliott's grandmother was getting fuzzy around the edges. "What does she do?"

"She sells houses," he said, putting his baseball hat on his head backward and banging the door shut behind him. He obviously thought he'd changed Maggie's mind and considered the matter closed. Maggie was glad to be warned about the Thanksgiving plans. She had a few days before Garrett came home for the weekend to practice her arguments against going to Grandma's house.

Garrett arrived Friday evening very much the way Elliott did after school—tired, dirty and full of talk. When Maggie looked out the front window at his tall figure emerging from the car she had to grip the edge of the couch to keep from running out to meet him. It would be so easy to throw her arms around him as Elliott did, to feel his arms tighten around her, the way it was with families all over the country.

But nannies stayed in the background, watching and waiting until they were called. Sometimes she wondered whom she was trying to convince that nannies had an ideal life, Garrett or herself.

Elliott had flung himself into Garrett's arms and Maggie could see the little boy talking a mile a minute. While she watched, Garrett looked up at the house and frowned. Without the lights on in the house, she didn't think he could see her, but she felt sure the frown had something to do with her.

He and Elliott came bounding up the front steps. "What's this about your not coming with us at Thanksgiving?" he asked, a cold wind blowing in with him.

He snapped on the lamp in the living room and studied her face. "Take my stuff back to the shed," he told Elliott, pointing to a toolbox and a duffel bag he'd left on the porch. Elliott looked reluctant to leave what promised to be an interesting conversation, but one look at his father's face convinced him to do as he was told.

Maggie decided that the best defense was a good offense. "What's this about my coming with you? I don't remember your having asked me." She moved to stand behind one of the chairs that flanked the fireplace, to put some space between them and to give her something to hold on to.

Garrett's hair was blown all over his head, his face was a deep tan and his eyes flashed.

"I told you we were going to Oregon. I told you how my mother had broken her hip, I'm sure I did."

"You told me you were going, you never said anything about me."

"When I say 'we' I mean you, too. I thought you knew that by now. Elliott expects you to go, I expect you to go and my mother expects you, too."

"Well, she'll just have to unexpect me, because I have other plans," Maggie said as firmly as she could under the full force of Garrett's disapproving gaze.

"To spend the day with a bunch of old, worn-out women who won't even notice if you're there or not? I never heard of anything so ridiculous."

Maggie squared her shoulders. "Wait just a minute. They are not old, worn-out women. They just happen to be professional women who enjoy each other's company, and most of all—" Maggie clenched her jaw "—most of all, appreciate the fact that they're free to do whatever they want on Thanksgiving *and* Christmas *and* New Year's. If you'll review our contract, I think you'll see that those are my prearranged holidays."

Garrett stared at her without speaking. Maybe she'd finally made an impression on him, after all. "Old, worn-out women." After all she'd said about being a nanny, it had obviously gone in one ear and out the other. He let out a long breath and sat down in a tall, straight-backed chair, calmer now, his anger under control.

"I see what the problem is," he said as if he were analyzing the algae in a trout pond. "The problem is that this is just a job to you, with a salary and paid vacations. And Elliott and I, we're just your employers, to be bargained with and treated just like bosses. But somewhere along the line I forgot about that and so did Elliott. And that's where we went wrong. We started thinking of you as part of the family, and we started to rely on you to be around when we needed you." He leaned forward in his chair. "And that's your fault, you know, because you've spoiled us."

Maggie blinked in surprise. "Garrett," she protested, "you hired me to take care of Elliott when you weren't here, and I've done that. I think I have been reliable, and I don't really think you're spoiled. But you've got to realize that I'm not a part of your family, and I still have a life of my own."

He appeared not to have heard her. "I don't know when it happened," he said, looking over her head and out the bay window. "Maybe it was that night when you helped me throw ice in the pond."

Maggie blushed and she pressed her spine into the back of the chair. How unfair of him to bring up that night.

"Or maybe it was the day you weighed fish, or when you fell asleep in the car coming back from Carmel . . . but somewhere along the line I stopped thinking of you as a nanny."

Maggie waited breathlessly to hear what he did think of her, but he just shook his head. "I don't have to review our contract. If you say you have Thanksgiving off, then you do. God knows we don't want you to go on strike."

Unnerved by his giving in so easily, Maggie managed to say "Thank you" without choking. She should have felt triumphant at having won the argument, but somehow she only felt let down and depressed at the thought of spending Thanksgiving without him. She wanted to say that she didn't think of him as an employer, either, that somewhere along the line she, too, had gone wrong, only she'd gone so far wrong she didn't know how she'd ever be right again. She realized with a jolt that somewhere along the line, she'd fallen in love with Garrett Townsend. And the thought left a hollow, helpless feeling in the pit of her stomach.

Maggie went through all the motions that weekend. Somehow she got through Friday night, cooking and serving and even eating dinner. Elliott was unusually quiet, as if his father had instructed him not to talk about Thanksgiving. Garrett was polite, but reserved. She caught him looking at her across the kitchen table, his expression serious, his eyes asking questions she didn't know how to answer.

After dinner Garrett and Elliott watched an old World War II movie on television and Maggie tried to sneak up to her room by taking her shoes off and padding quietly behind the couch they were sitting on. But Garrett turned around just as she reached the bottom step.

"Good night," he called loudly over the sound of the gunfire coming from the screen.

Maggie waved and stepped lightly up the stairs to her room. He was still angry with her and maybe even embarrassed that he'd told everyone she was going with them before he'd asked her, and she wasn't making things easy by sticking to her plans.

Saturday was her day off and she got up early and drove off before they woke up. There was a fine mist in the air blowing in off the coast, which suited her mood and she figured there wouldn't be many customers at the trout farm today. They would get along fine without her. So fine, in fact, that Garrett would realize he'd made a scene over nothing. They'd spent Thanksgivings without her in the past, and they'd spend many Thanksgivings without her in the future.

The thought made her eyes mist over and she turned on the windshield wipers, not even realizing she was crying.

She stopped for breakfast in Half Moon Bay and dawdled until the shopping center was open on the other side of the hill. She intended to buy a dress for Thanksgiving, something urban and sophisticated, just to prove to herself that she was going to Mrs. Newcastle's and to make it impossible to change her mind. Once she had the dress, she'd have to go.

She found it too easily. There it was on a mannequin in the window with Maggie written all over it, a deep plum-colored wool that clung to the bodice and flared below the hips. The saleswoman told her it was her color, and Maggie saw that it was. It made her cheeks glow and her eyes shine and made Maggie feel like kicking up the heels of the new shoes she bought to go with it.

Then she wandered through the stores looking at things she wished she could buy for Garrett, like socks that matched and shirts without stains, and books and toys she would like to buy for Elliott for Christmas. Even though she didn't know where she'd be on Christmas, she bought a few presents for Elliott and some yarn and a pattern to make a sweater for Garrett. The yarn was a sea green and it looked like him. But even so, she could always change her mind and turn it into a scarf for her grandmother. A sweater was really too personal a gift from a nanny to her employer.

Maggie went to a movie in the evening and drove home slowly through the rain, hoping that they'd have gone to bed by the time she got there. But Garrett was waiting for her at the front door. Deep creases were in his forehead.

"Have a nice time?" he asked, watching her come through the door.

"Great," she lied.

"We missed you," he said, keeping his eyes on her as she reached down to take off her wet shoes.

She straightened. "Why, did you have a lot of customers? I thought it would be a slow day."

"It was a slow day. It went on and on, and it isn't over yet. Sit down—I'll make you some coffee. Or how about some cocoa, that's what Elliott had."

"All right." Maggie sat down on the couch and drew her legs underneath her. When Garrett went into the kitchen she shook the rain out of her hair and leaned her head back against the wall. It had been a long day for her too, trying to fill in the hours of a day off she didn't want. She had put some space between herself and Garrett, though, and that was reason enough to take a day off. Now she just had to get through Sunday and he would be gone again on Monday.

He handed her a cup of hot chocolate and stood over her while she sipped it until her hand shook and the cup rattled in the saucer. What did he want with her?

He walked to the fireplace and leaned on the mantel, nudging the picture of Elliott and his soccer team with his elbow.

"I'm sorry I said what I said about nannies. I know you're good at what you do and I know you enjoy it, but I can't get it through my head why somebody like you, who's got so much to give, who's so good with kids..." he paused and looked down at his scuffed running shoes then back into her eyes, "wouldn't want to be married and have kids of her own."

He drew his shoulders up and raised his hands in a helpless gesture, as if all in the world he wanted was to understand what made her tick. It was almost enough to make her jump up and tell him the whole story and end up by admitting that she'd gone the way of all the nannies she'd ever read about and fallen in love with her employer.

Instead of turning out like her role model, Mary Poppins, who was blessed with a stiff upper lip, she felt she was losing what little willpower she had left. The sagging cushions on the couch, the hot drink spreading warmth through her body and Garrett's dark eyes on her made it impossible to play any games.

She took a deep breath and moved away from the soft cushions to the edge of the couch. Garrett had been straightforward with her, maybe too much so, but it was time for her to set the record straight.

"I did want those things—getting married and having children. I wanted them so badly that I rushed into marriage as soon as I finished college. I even majored in nutrition and minored in early childhood education. Nobody was more prepared. Nobody wanted kids more than I did. That's why..." Maggie swallowed hard. "That's why..." If only he wouldn't look at her that way, with a mixture of alarm and sympathy. "That's why I won't ever do it again."

Garrett sat down on the raised tile hearth around the fireplace and crossed his arms. "It didn't work out?" he asked gently.

"It was all wrong, from the beginning to the end," she admitted sadly.

"Maybe it was just the wrong person," he suggested.

"The wrong person was me." Maggie shrugged as if it weren't important anymore. "I just wasn't good at it." She said it lightly as if marriage were a game that some people were good at and others weren't. She wasn't fooling herself, but maybe Garrett.

He eased himself down onto the floor until his head rested on the tile hearth, and he was flat on his back. He stared at the ceiling.

"What about children?"

"I wasn't good at that, either," she confessed, hoping he wouldn't ask for any details. Three miscarriages in three years, prognosis, unfavorable. She stood up quickly. "So there you have it, the story of my life, the reason I became a nanny. The reason I'm here today."

Garrett didn't move. Maybe the story had put him to sleep. With him lying there on the floor, she couldn't tell. Maggie tiptoed to the fireplace and looked down at him. His eyes were squeezed shut, deep ridges ran across his deep forehead. Even when he slept his lower lip jutted out. Even when he slept he looked stubborn.

And even when he slept she felt a current flow between them and she knew he felt it, too. It was the reason he'd kissed her in the kitchen the day she'd baked apples and the night she told his fortune, and it was the reason he looked at her the way he did over a fishhook or the Sunday morning breakfast table.

It was an attraction they both felt and that they both fought. Suddenly Garrett's hands shot up and grabbed Maggie's hands and pulled her down on her knees next to him on the floor.

"I thought you were asleep," she gasped.

Garrett shook his head. "Just thinking about you." He held her hands together in his and closed his eyes again. She felt the warmth from his fingers spread from her hands all the way to her heart and melt the cold wall of resentment she'd built when she learned about his Thanksgiving plans. It seemed impossible for her to stay angry with Garrett for longer than twenty-four hours, no matter what he did, and she didn't know how to account for that.

She looked at his face, studying the way his hair fell across his wide forehead, noticing the way his thick eyebrows made him look skeptical, even when he was stretched out flat on the floor. Her gaze lingered on his mouth. In spite of her resolve, she remembered the way he'd kissed her in the fortune-teller's booth, as if he couldn't stop himself.

What if, just once, he kissed her the way she wanted to be kissed, slowly, deliberately, as if he had all the time in the world, as if he knew that was what she wanted?

Maggie squeezed her eyelids together and pulled her hands from out of his. Enough of living in a fantasy world. Garrett Townsend was Elliott's father and her employer. He was also a man with normal instincts. He would probably be attracted to any woman under fifty who came to live in his house and was always available.

"About Thanksgiving..." Garrett began.

"That's what I was thinking about," Maggie lied.

"Then you'll come?" He sat up and tilted her chin forward with his thumb.

Maggie sighed and wiggled across the floor away from him. When Garrett turned on his persistence and looked at her as if she were a national treasure, she didn't know how long she could continue to resist.

"Tell me again why you'll need me up there," she said, trying to remember if he had ever told her.

"Well," he propped his head in his hand, "there's my mother. She's old, you know, and Elliott might be too much for her."

Maggie frowned. "Too much?"

He nodded vigorously. "Too much noise, uh, commotion. You know how old people are. She lives alone. She's not used to having him around." He paused. "Not that she doesn't like him. She's crazy about him, but three days is a long time. So sometimes you could take him to the park or something." He grinned at Maggie and she felt the corners of her mouth turning up in response.

She gave it one more try. "But you'll be there, Garrett. Why couldn't you take him to the park if he gets to be too much?"

"Me?" He closed his eyes for a moment. "Because there are things I have to discuss with my mother, family matters, you know."

I know, she thought, I know only too well that you're pushing me, and that if you keep it up, I'll cave in under the pressure. But all of a sudden the prospect of a sophisticated Thanksgiving with soft music and a maid who served turkey from a silver tray didn't seem very appealing.

"So what do you say, Maggie? Give us a chance. Then, if you don't have a good time, I won't make you go next year."

"Next year? Garrett, there won't be a next year. I'm temporary, remember?"

"I remember. That's why we have to make the most of every moment, every holiday, right?"

Maggie nodded slowly. "Right," she admitted reluctantly. Actually she didn't know if it was right or not. But she knew where she was going to spend Thanksgiving. And it wasn't at Mrs. Newcastle's.

Maggie didn't win the turkey at the school raffle, but she didn't know what she would have done with it if she had. It wouldn't have fit under her seat on the small, commuter airplane that took them to Ashland, Oregon, the day before Thanksgiving. And she could imagine the look on Garrett's mother's face as she handed the elderly woman a twenty-two-pound turkey.

Mrs. Townsend was surprised enough just to see Maggie. Maggie wondered what she had expected. No one at all? Someone much older? Garrett's mother surveyed Maggie with wide brown eyes, shadowed with purple and lined with brown, shifting her adoring gaze from Garrett to Elliott and then back to Maggie who was trying to hide in the backseat of the car.

"You'll have to forgive me for staring." Garrett's mother's eyes met Maggie's in the rearview mirror. "But I've never seen a nanny before."

Garrett turned his head to give Maggie an encouraging grin and even Elliott, sitting beside her, tilted his head to smile at her.

All the unaccustomed attention caught Maggie off guard. It was better not to say anything, she decided, until she figured out what was on Garrett's mother's mind. She didn't have to wait long. Once inside the spacious frame house, Garrett's mother sent Elliott and Garrett out to play football, motioned Maggie to a chair at the kitchen table, poured her a cup of instant coffee and told Maggie to call her Dorothy.

"I was surprised when Garrett first told me he'd hired a nanny." Dorothy slid her trim black leather pants onto the chair across from Maggie. "I mean, why would a real nanny want to work on an old, broken-down fish farm?" Dorothy looked at Maggie through yellow-tinted glasses that twirled up at the corners. "Why did you?"

Rather than go into her speech about the rewards of taking care of other people's children, Maggie shook her head. "I didn't," she admitted. "It was a mistake, a mix-up back at the agency. But now that I'm there..." Maggie trailed off. What could she say? *Now that I'm there I've fallen in love with your son and become so attached to your grandson I want to stay forever?* She tried again. "Now that I'm there, I've gotten used to the place. And Elliott's a wonderful child." That part was true, and any grandmother would have to agree.

Dorothy nodded. Then she picked up her coffee cup and studied it thoughtfully. "But I imagine Garrett isn't easy to live with."

Maggie took a quick sip of coffee. "But I don't live with him, really. I mean he's hardly ever there, so it's not like that."

"Then he's behaving himself?"

Maggie pretended not to understand the question, but she made the mistake of glancing up at Dorothy and blushing.

"I see," Dorothy murmured, stirring her coffee absently. "Well, I'm glad you came. This way we get a chance to know each other before..." She hesitated and Maggie wondered what she wanted to say. Before you leave? Or before it's too late?

"I don't like surprises," she said, "so if anything's going on between you and Garrett, I'd like to know. If I'd known about Helena, I could have said something. That woman had disaster written all over her." She looked hard at Maggie as if she were trying to read what she had written all over her.

Maggie shifted uneasily in her chair, then she looked straight at Dorothy and met her gaze. "Garrett and I have a business relationship. He needs a nanny for Elliott and I need a job." Maggie was beginning to feel like a broken record, singing the same song over and over. If only the words didn't sound so empty when she said them. She tried again. "I admit I've become attached to Elliott, but it would be unprofessional of me to form any sort of attachment to Garrett. So you don't have to worry about me turning into another Helena."

Dorothy shook her head. "Oh, you're nothing like her. Nothing, at all. She was a stunning looking woman." She raised her eyebrows above her glasses. "Just stunning."

Maggie bit her lower lip and felt decidedly unstunning.

"I can't help worrying about my son," Dorothy continued, looking past Maggie to the windows that faced the fenced-in yard where Garrett and Elliott were playing ball. "When you have children you'll understand."

Maggie's heart fell. She didn't need to come all the way to Oregon to be reminded that she didn't have children and never would.

"Understand what?" Garrett stood in the doorway, his cheeks bright red and his sweatshirt streaked with dirt. Why had he brought her here? Maggie wondered, and wished she'd never come. At least at Mrs. Newcastle's she wouldn't have been compared to anyone's first wife or been reminded of her inability to have children.

"Understand how a mother worries about her children." Dorothy picked up their coffee cups, her silver bracelets jangling against each other.

Maggie felt her nerve endings jangle and she gritted her teeth. If Garrett had brought her here to get his mother's approval, she could leave right now. In the space of a few minutes Dorothy had made her feel both unworthy and unattractive.

Garrett frowned at the sight of Maggie's pale face. She brushed past him on her way out the door, saying she was going to play catch with Elliott.

Garrett leaned against the dining-room wall and surveyed his mother with narrow eyes. "What were you and Maggie talking about?"

She looked up innocently. "Oh, just the usual—men, women and children." She stood up and looked at her watch. "I have an appointment to show a house at one."

Garrett moved to block the doorway. "Maggie means a lot to me, Mother."

"I can see that. I just don't want to see you make another mistake."

"Wait a minute. Maggie is not another Helena."

"She certainly isn't."

"Maggie is the most warmhearted, unselfish person I've ever met," Garrett said firmly.

"I'm sure she is."

"Then why don't you like her?" Garrett asked, folding his arms across his chest.

His mother stood up. "I do like her. But I'm not sure she's your type."

Garrett felt like banging his head against a wall. His mother had been this way every time he'd ever brought a girl home. Why had he thought it would be different this time? It wasn't.

"What is my type, Mother?" he asked patiently.

She squinted at him through her glasses. "I don't know. Glamorous, maybe, dashing and adventurous."

"Uh-uh. Not anymore." He looked out the window at Maggie backing into the bushes to chase a ball. "That's my type out there." It was true. All those years up to and including Helena he'd been chasing the wrong kind of woman. His luck had changed when Maggie walked up the front steps to his house. He couldn't imagine living without her. Some day he would have to, but for the moment he didn't want to think about it.

His mother changed the subject. "What about that land you were interested in on the river?"

"I put a bid on it but they turned me down."

She raised her eyebrows in surprise. "And now what?"

"I don't know. That depends. I could make another offer. But there are complications." His gaze drifted to the window where Maggie was throwing the ball to Elliott. "How's your hip?" he asked abruptly, "I hope it hasn't kept you out of your bowling league."

She smiled. "We have a game tonight, as a matter of fact, and the doctor says I can do anything I like. I was going to cancel, because you're here, but they said Elliott could come with me. Everyone wants to meet my wonderful grandson. But you and Maggie—"

"Have other plans." Garrett finished her sentence for her.

His mother shrugged and raised her hands. Was it a graceful gesture of defeat or just a temporary truce? Garrett stepped aside and she walked through the doorway, into the kitchen and out to the garage to get her car and go to her appointment.

By five o'clock that night, it was dark enough to turn on all the lights. But after his mother and Elliott left the house for the bowling alley, Garrett went around turning them off. He built a fire in the fireplace. Garrett could understand his mother's disapproving of Helena, but anyone with two eyes ought to be able to see how Maggie glowed with her own special brand of quiet sex appeal.

Sitting across the card table from her in front of the blazing fireplace he could see it clearer than ever. Glamorous, dashing and adventurous? Who needed it? Not Maggie. She was perfect the way she was.

She looked up at him over a plate of steaming linguine with clam sauce, her lips curved in a smile of approval. "Garrett, this is good. How did you make it?"

He smiled modestly. "Specialty of the house. An old family secret." He stood up, reached for the bottle of white wine on the mantel and filled her glass. "I didn't give you a choice about what you wanted to do tonight. I hope you didn't want to go bowling."

Maggie shook her head and looked down at her plate. Her eyelashes made shadows on her pink cheeks and Garrett reached for her hand under the table. Her fingers returned the pressure and his heart pounded. Maybe for a few days, or even a few hours, she could forget she was a nanny. He already had. He knew he shouldn't, but he was only human.

"You don't really need me here this weekend, do you?" she asked, meeting his gaze with her wide hazel eyes. "I mean Elliott has you and his grandmother and me. I wonder why you brought me."

"Need you?" he asked incredulously. "I always need you. I thought you knew that. It must be my fault. I haven't made you feel needed and wanted."

"You have, but—"

"My mother hasn't, has she?"

"I don't think she likes me. She was appraising me as if I were an old house, one that was overpriced and not very well built. It doesn't matter, of course."

Garrett smiled at her description. "That's right, it doesn't."

"After all, I didn't come here to get her approval." She twirled noodles around her fork and frowned at them. "Why did I come here?"

Garrett put his hands on the table. "You came because I wanted you to come. Because I want you around. Because . . ." He fumbled, afraid to say too much. "Because I miss you when you're not around," he blurted.

Her lips parted as if she were going to say something, but she just shook her head, her hair swinging against her cheek.

After a long moment he finally spoke again, "Obviously you don't feel the same way." He tried to keep his voice matter-of-fact, but the disappointment gave him a tight feeling in his chest.

"Maybe if we had met under different circumstances," Maggie suggested in a strained voice, "we'd have a better idea of how we feel about each other. Living in the same house has thrown us together, but it's an abnormal situation. It's made us more aware of each other than we should be."

"What are you saying?" Garrett stood up and circled the table, feeling the adrenaline pumping through his body. "That we start all over again? That we pretend we haven't eaten and slept together? How are people supposed to meet each other then—on blind dates or at bars? Those are the abnormal situations." He looked around the room. "Not these."

Maggie pushed her chair away from the table and looked up at Garrett. "If you're talking about that night in the tent, don't you mean 'slept next to each other'?"

"I am talking about that night in the tent and I do not mean slept next to each other, because I did not sleep at all that night. I couldn't, with you lying next to me. I wanted to unzip your sleeping bag and take you into mine, but I didn't do anything about it because I knew you wouldn't like it, and now I'm sorry because it looks like I'll never get another chance." Garrett broke off at the sight of Maggie's shocked expression. Her eyes were so bright they could have burned holes right through him, but her mouth trembled as if she were going to cry.

He held his arms out to her and for one moment he thought she might come to him, until he heard the front door open.

"Another chance for what?" his mother asked, stowing her bowling bag in the hall closet.

"Another chance to go bowling," Garrett said without turning around. He kept his eyes on Maggie as he reached for Elliott and held him by the shoulders.

"How did you do?" he asked him.

"He was the star of the team," his mother assured him. Her sweeping gaze took in the smoldering fire, the empty plates and the wineglasses and finally rested on Maggie who was twisting her napkin in her hands.

"I hope I haven't interrupted anything," Garrett's mother said sweetly. "I would have knocked or rung the bell, but Maggie assured me your relationship was strictly business."

"That's right." Maggie stood up and Garrett cringed. Here it comes, he thought, her nanny speech.

"I take my job seriously." Maggie carefully piled the dinner dishes one on top of another, and Garrett thought, you can say that again. "But that doesn't mean that I don't enjoy what I'm doing. Garrett and Elliott have made me feel wanted, as if I belonged with them. Which I don't," she added, looking at Garrett. "Garrett's my employer, and sometimes it's hard for me to remember that. Coming here has been good for me." She looked straight at his mother. "It's made me aware of who I am and who I'm not." She smiled grimly and walked into the kitchen with the dishes.

"I did interrupt something, didn't I?" Garrett's mother switched on the overhead light and looked at him.

He stood up slowly and ran his hand through his hair. "It's all right, it's your house. But, Mother..."

"Yes?"

"Next time knock."

"Of course. If there is a next time. Tomorrow we'll be having dinner at the country club. That way I can write it off as a business expense. There's always someone there who's looking for a house."

There was the sound of water running in the kitchen. "Up to bed, Elliott," Garrett ordered. "I'm going to dry the dishes, if it's not too late."

His mother gave an exaggerated yawn and took Elliott by the hand. "Elliott and I are exhausted. I hope Maggie will understand if I go straight up to bed. Say good-night to her for me, won't you?"

"I'll do that." Garrett pushed the kitchen door open.

Maggie was washing dishes at the kitchen sink, and he could tell by the set of her shoulders she was tense. He cleared his throat, but she didn't turn around.

He walked up behind her and put his hands on her shoulder blades, massaging them gently. "Where were we before we were interrupted?" he breathed into her ear. The smell of detergent mingled with the smell of Maggie's hair, the familiar flower scent that clung to her and reminded him of the first night she'd spent in his house, the night she came downstairs in her nightgown looking like an enchantress and bewitching him with her magic.

She didn't stop washing dishes, but he noticed with satisfaction that she seemed to have slowed down a little.

"I don't remember," she answered.

"I do. We were discussing whether we'd slept next to each other or not," he said lightly. He let his hands slide down her arms and she finally took her hands out of the soapy water and dried them on her apron. "Wasn't that it?"

She twisted around to face him. "It's no good, Garrett, pretending everything is all right. You and I are not meant to have anything but a business arrangement."

Garrett kept his hands on her arms and his eyes on her troubled face. "How do you know that? Did you see it in your crystal ball?"

A corner of her mouth almost lifted in a smile. "I don't need a crystal ball to see that your mother doesn't like me. We don't live our lives in a vacuum. We're connected to our parents and our children and that's the way it should be. You can say it doesn't matter what your mother thinks, but it does."

"Of course it does. I don't deny that. But here's the way it works. Funny I never noticed it before. When I brought Helena home, Mother thought she was wild and unpredictable, and started comparing her with some girlfriend I'd had in college." He shook his head and shrugged his shoulders.

Maggie studied his face and he brought his hand up and gently outlined her cheek with one finger.

"And now that I'm here on the scene, Helena doesn't look so bad anymore. Is that what you mean?"

Garrett nodded. "Exactly."

"And when the next woman comes along, maybe your mother will appreciate me. But I don't think I can wait around for it to happen."

Garrett dropped his hands to his sides. "There isn't going to be any next woman," he said quietly. He knew with a sudden certainty that it was true.

"How can you say that?"

"It's easy. There isn't going to be anyone else. Ever." For one magical second the look in her eyes told him she believed him. Then her gaze faltered and terrible doubts shook him. "Unless," he continued, "unless you don't want what I want." And even if she did...The doubts continued to batter away at him. Was it fair to take another chance on forever? If he'd learned anything at all, it was that there were no guarantees.

Maggie shook her head. "I don't know what I want anymore. Maybe when we get home I'll be able to think clearly again."

Garrett nodded. She didn't know it, but she'd said "home" as if it really were her home. He picked up a dish towel and reached for a plate. He would hang on to that shred of hope. It was all he had for now.

Chapter Eight

Back home everything was the same, but visions of Maggie were forever imprinted in Garrett's memory. She had looked beautiful in a plum-colored dress at the country club. Heads turned when she went to the buffet table to choose her dessert, and Garrett noticed that his mother noticed. During the rest of the weekend while his mother wrote up offers and counteroffers, Maggie, Garrett and Elliott took walks in the park, kicking up golden-brown leaves as they went looking for the children's playground.

And while his mother was out showing houses, the three of them went to a movie and out for pizza. Garrett didn't say anything about anything that mattered, and he was rewarded by seeing the worry lines around Maggie's mouth disappear. He even heard her laugh from time to time at the things Elliott said.

Maggie too was relieved to be back home, although she knew it was presumptuous of her to think of it as home, she didn't know what else to call it. She looked around at the kitchen one Sunday morning, at the familiar cracks in the linoleum floor and at Elliott's drawings of fighter planes that were stuck to the refrigerator door with magnets and she knew she wouldn't trade it for the most luxurious town house in San Francisco. Not yet, anyway. Not until she had to.

"Maggie looks as if she doesn't believe you," Garrett was saying to Elliott, and Maggie looked up inquiringly from her bowl of oatmeal. "Or maybe she's just not listening."

"You've never seen Big Lou, have you Maggie?" Elliott took his jacket from a hook next to the back door.

"Who's that, your forty-pound fish?"

Elliott nodded.

"I haven't seen him, but that doesn't mean I don't believe he exists. I've never seen the Loch Ness monster either or Big Foot, but I believe in them."

Elliott shook his head in disgust. "Come on, Maggie. Big Lou isn't like that. He's real. He's this long." He held his jacket in his teeth while he stretched his arms out wide. Then he went outside in the bright December sunshine and let the door slam behind him.

"Big Lou is so real," Garrett turned to face her from the kitchen sink, "that I'm offering a twenty-five-dollar reward to anyone who catches him."

"Twenty-five dollars?" Maggie stirred her oatmeal thoughtfully. "I'm tempted to try to catch him myself."

"Sorry." He picked up a sponge and squeezed it dry. "This offer is void, prohibited and restricted. Not available to members of the Townsend family."

Maggie put her spoon down and stood up. He wasn't going to go through this member of the family business again, was he? Just as she was about to remind him she wasn't a member of the family, he added an afterthought.

"Or employees of Townsend's Trout Farm." He wiped the counter with the clean sponge. "Come on outside— maybe you'll get a look at him before everyone gets here."

He held the back door open for her, and Maggie's heart lurched as she brushed against him on her way out. Ever since they'd come back from Oregon, Garrett hadn't mentioned the property. His supplier went bankrupt, so he spent the weekdays looking for a new hatchery to supply the trout farm with fingerlings. He left early every morning before she woke up, and came home late and did calculations at the kitchen table.

She certainly couldn't fault him on his behavior. He hadn't made any personal remarks or talked about the future. He hadn't touched her or even looked at her with that special glint in his eye. Maybe it was because he was hardly ever there. She told herself she was glad. She told herself it was a relief.

Maggie snuck a sideways glance at him and wondered what had brought about the change in their relationship. Maybe Garrett, too, realized that Helena far outshone her in looks and glamour, ambition and drive. Those might not be qualifications for motherhood, but they sounded pretty romantic.

Garrett spotted some customers on the other side of the pond and took off at a sprint. Maggie stared into the murky waters of the pond at her reflection. Straight hair, no makeup, an old sweatshirt and jeans. She threw a pebble in the water and watched her reflection dissolve into waves. No wonder Garrett was leaving her alone.

"Did you see him?" Elliott's face appeared next to her reflection.

"Nope. He's probably hiding at the bottom. I would, wouldn't you? I guess it's time to go to work." She took his hand. "Did you come to get me?"

They walked over to the entrance together and with the scale and the cash register between them, worked steadily all morning. Garrett's advertising campaign seemed to have worked. Customers came in droves, but nobody caught Big Lou, if there really was a Big Lou.

Maggie ran into Garrett in the bait shack in the late afternoon. He stepped over a flat of night crawlers and reached for a net in the corner, steadying himself with one hand on her shoulder.

His touch set off such a strong longing to feel his arms around her that she had to say something, anything to break the spell.

"Any luck?"

"Not yet," he answered keeping his hand on her shoulder. "But catching fish takes patience, and knowing what you're after." He looked at her intently. "I know what I'm after, Maggie. Do you?"

As if to answer his question Maggie leaned her head to one side, to feel his hand against her cheek. He dropped the net on the floor and stared into her eyes. With one hand on either side of her face he drew her to him. Her heart fluttered wildly. Voices outside blended and faded away. His lips touched hers and the hunger she felt in him matched her own.

The rumble of voices outside rose and reached a crescendo and matched the pounding of Maggie's heart. Garrett pulled away from her, his eyes glazed with desire. "Did you hear something?" he asked looking around. He pushed open the door and Maggie followed him outside.

A little girl about Elliott's age wearing striped overalls was holding a fishing rod almost bent in half by the weight of an enormous fish.

"Big Lou?" Maggie murmured to herself. How could it be anything else? A man who must have been her father tried to take the rod from the child, but stubbornly she gripped it even tighter. Maggie pushed her way through the crowd and watched Garrett approach the girl with the fish.

Gently Garrett removed the hook from the fish's mouth and placed the huge trout in the child's arms. She looked up at him, her eyes wide with surprise, and staggered backward with the weight of the fish.

People around Maggie clapped and whistled. Garrett's eyes found Maggie in the crowd.

"Get my camera," he shouted.

"Where is it?" she shouted back.

He shook his head and motioned for her to take his place at the little girl's side. "Never mind, I'll get it. You stay here and take care of Big Lou."

Maggie nodded and looked down at the huge fish and the girl who held it, and saw her face shine with excitement. Behind her stood her father beaming with pride. Her mother was kneeling next to her looking anxious. Probably wondering who was going to clean and cook all that fish, Maggie thought. On Maggie's other side, Elliott grabbed her arm.

"See, Maggie, see? I told you, I told you he was real." Elliott squirmed with delight. Maggie watched him with fond amusement just a second too long. When she turned back, Big Lou, with a mighty thrust, was hurling himself back into the water. The little girl and her mother screamed and jumped back to avoid the splash, and "ooooh's" reverberated through the crowd.

"That's *my* fish." The child's face contorted with grief and tears squeezed from her eyes. With a stamp of her little foot she stepped to the edge of the pond and jumped in after Big Lou.

Maggie gasped and without thinking jumped in after her. The water hit her with a shock, and her feet sunk into the mud at the bottom. She hadn't realized it was so cold or so shallow. She walked through the dark brown, muddy water with agonizing slowness to where the child was flailing her arms about. Maggie picked her up and held her tightly against her chest. She was cold and wet and heavy, and Maggie made soothing noises in her ear.

"I want my fish," she screamed. Maggie looked around for Big Lou, but wet strands of hair fell forward into her face blocking her vision.

"I don't know where he is," she admitted helplessly. As she approached the sloping cement edge of the pond she saw Garrett leaning forward, his arms outstretched, his camera swinging from around his neck. She thought briefly that scenes like this were not the kind to encourage people to try their luck at Townsend's Trout Farm.

She held the child out and Garrett lifted her up to her parents who hugged her between them.

He turned back to Maggie, still standing waist-deep in the water. "What happened?" he asked with an irritated frown. "I thought I told you to watch him."

"I was," she sputtered. "I looked away just for a second and he was gone."

He reached down to pull her up, but Maggie felt too angry to take his hands. He thought it was her fault. She could tell by the look on his face. She folded her arms across her chest. "There was nothing anybody could do to stop him. That fish just didn't want to be caught."

"No fish wants to be caught. I could have told you that." He glared at her. "Are you coming out of there?"

"Maybe you'd like me to look around for him first," Maggie suggested sarcastically. She hadn't taken care of Big Lou, it was true, but Garrett was acting as if she'd let Moby Dick slip away.

Garrett reached down and grabbed Maggie around the waist with both hands. "I'd like you to get out of that water," he said forcefully.

Maggie pulled out of his grasp and pulled herself up out of the pond, her hands gripping the cold cement. She stood on wobbly legs, and with as much dignity as she could manage with blue jeans slapping against her legs and her cold, soggy sweatshirt clinging to her body, she walked back to the house.

From the shelf in the bathroom she took a large towel and sloshed her way back out to the parking lot in search of the little girl.

"There she is." The mother waved to Maggie, her expression one of relief and gratitude. "You're the lady who saved my baby. You were wonderful. I panicked. Honestly, I couldn't move. I felt like I was frozen to the spot."

Maggie held up the bath towel and the mother peeled the wet clothes off the child and wrapped her in the towel, holding her close. She looked up at Maggie.

"How can we ever thank you? Can you say thank you, Jessica?"

Jessica shook her head and Maggie smiled understandingly. Garrett wasn't the only one who was disappointed in her performance. But the child's father clasped Maggie's hands in his. "You deserve a medal. I don't know what was wrong with the rest of us, but you were in the water before I knew what had happened."

"It was pure instinct." Maggie looked down at her wet feet and shivered.

The child's mother looked concerned. "You'd better get into some dry clothes before you catch your death," she admonished Maggie. The little girl gave Maggie one last mournful look before they got into their car, the parents still praising Maggie's courage and resourcefulness as they pulled away.

Maggie turned and almost bumped into Garrett. Had he heard how wonderful they thought she was? She marched purposefully past him without looking at him, her feet squishing in her soggy running shoes. She went back to the house for the second time. She didn't know if she was shaking with cold or anger as she changed into a dry shirt and pants.

She was determined to return to the pond to finish the day, but when she looked out her bedroom window she saw Garrett and Elliott locking the gate. She realized it must be almost five o'clock. She pulled back the blankets on her bed and lay down. Even under three blankets and a flannel sheet, she continued to shiver.

She heard footsteps in the kitchen and the back door slammed shut.

"Maggie?" she heard Elliott shout. When she answered her voice came out like a croak.

Two sets of footsteps tromped up the stairs and Maggie wished she could have brushed her hair. With her hand, she could feel it had dried in a tangled mess. They burst into her room.

"What happened to you all of a sudden? Why did you disappear just when everybody wanted to thank you?" Garrett asked.

"They did thank me," Maggie assured him, "but there was no need to. I was just doing my job."

Elliott sat on one side of her bed and Garrett on the other, hemming her in. "Is that what you call it?" Garrett asked.

"Of course. Any nanny would have done the same. We have emergency training. It's all right there in the Nanny's 'Water Safety Manual.'"

Garrett looked around the room, then down at his watch and back at Maggie. "What are you doing in bed at this hour, anyway? You look terrible."

"I feel terrible. I can't seem to get warm."

Elliott's eyes widened. "Poor Maggie. What are we having for dinner?"

"Elliott." Garrett frowned at him. "You and I are making dinner for Maggie. Some hot broth and some tea and toast. I have a feeling that's what Mary Poppins would prescribe, wouldn't she?"

"Something hot," Maggie murmured, closing her eyes.

Elliott jumped up. "I can make the toast," he announced and ran out of the room.

Garrett put his large, rough hand against Maggie's forehead, and she sighed. He cleared his throat. "I'm sorry if I seemed, uh, ungrateful out there. It was a shock. You in the water, the little girl and . . ."

"And no Lou," she finished his sentence.

"No Lou," he said matter-of-factly, his hand moving to her cheekbone, then to her chin. "But as I was saying out there in the shed, catching the big one requires time and patience and I've got both."

Maggie kept her eyes shut and she felt him lean over, felt his warm breath on her lips, his hand cool against her fevered cheek.

"Is it worth it?" Maggie was afraid to open her eyes. She wanted to lie there forever and feel Garrett's hand on her

MAKE ROOM FOR NANNY

131

face, his fingers tracing her cheek down to the indentation in her throat.

"Is it worth waiting to get what you want?" Garrett repeated the question for himself as much as Maggie. And suddenly he knew the answer. It was so obvious. "Of course," he said, urgently, "and you and I want the same thing." He put his hands under her pillow and lifted her head up to face him.

Maggie's face flamed and her pulse raced. Was it delirium or was it love? In the early stages they felt the same. His cheek was against hers now, cool and rough and smelling like the wind off the ocean. He was holding her, surrounding her with his strength, his mouth against her ear.

"We do, Maggie, listen to me." Take it slow, Garrett told himself. This was going to be too much for her, too much too soon. He'd been thinking about it for months, what to do about Maggie. And now that it had fallen into place, it seemed so natural, so right, so inevitable. But it might not seem that way to her, not at first.

He took a deep breath. "I know being a nanny is a noble profession, but for you it's just the beginning, not the end. Elliott and I need you more than anybody else ever will, and not just temporarily. We're going to have a whole new life with room to grow, and room for our children. Don't you want to be a part of that new life?"

He watched her move her lips, but no sound came out. Her eyelids flickered and closed. Had she heard him? If she had, what would she have said? He eased her head onto the pillow and watched her sleep.

Maggie heard the words, but she didn't know what they meant. She tried to answer, but no words came. He had asked her something, something important, but she couldn't keep her eyes open. She drifted away, still in his arms but on a different level of consciousness.

She woke up when the tea and toast came, sipped a little tea and fell asleep again.

In the morning she didn't wake up until it was light and she squinted at her alarm clock. Someone had turned it off, and the house was quiet. Who had gotten Elliott off to school? She stood up and coughed and lay down and coughed some more. From her window she could see Garrett's car was still in the driveway.

It was funny, but nobody had ever told her what to do when the nanny got sick. She knew what to do for sick children, it was all there in the manual. She didn't know anything about adult diseases, although if a child had a sore throat, cough, chills and fever, she'd put him to bed and take his temperature and keep him on liquids, just as she was doing to herself.

She stood up. She had to find Garrett and tell him she was all right, so he could go back to work on the river. There were footsteps in the kitchen and then on the stairs. She opened her door and he stood there in a soft flannel shirt tucked into his usual tight, faded jeans.

"Where do you think you're going?" he asked and led her back to bed.

"I was coming to find you. I'm fine. You can leave now. I can manage."

"That's not what the doctor said."

"What doctor?"

"The one I just called. They don't make house calls, but they give advice over the phone."

Garrett lifted her feet off the floor and swung them under the blankets. He looked at her shirt and pants, the same ones she'd changed into yesterday after she jumped into the water.

"I think you ought to be wearing a nightgown. You're not going anywhere, you know. Where is it? I'll get it for you."

Maggie pointed to her dresser drawer. He almost thought for a moment that Maggie was going to take off her shirt and pants and then he'd let the nightgown float gently over her body. It was so tantalizingly easy to picture. She took the nightgown from his hands but she didn't take her clothes off.

"What do you mean, I'm not going anywhere? What did the doctor say?"

"He said to keep you in bed for a few days and watch you." He sat on the edge of the bed and looked at her. "So that's what I'm doing."

Maggie's cheeks were pale and her nose was red. She looked as if she hadn't slept for days, even though that was all she had been doing, and he felt a surge of protectiveness. Maggie, the protector, the care-giver, needed taking care of. He'd never seen her down before, and it touched him. She needed him. For once she needed him, he realized with a jolt. It wouldn't last, but he'd make the most of it. But he wouldn't take advantage of her weakness to ask her again to share his life. He'd wait until she was well and she could think rationally. He'd waited all these months. He could wait a little longer.

She leaned back on her pillow.

"How are we feeling?" he asked, his palm on her forehead.

"Fine." She smiled weakly.

"Hungry?"

She shook her head.

"I think we'd better eat something anyway. Got to keep our strength up."

Maggie squinted at him through half-opened eyes. "Is that what the doctor said?"

"That's what I say." He quickly leaned over and kissed her on the forehead before she knew what he was doing. When he came back with a tray she was wearing her nightgown and she managed a faint smile.

It wasn't the same floaty nightgown she'd worn the night she arrived, but it reminded him of that magic night. He wished he could start all over again. How could he have been so paranoid as to tell her not to answer the door? She must have thought he was crazy.

How much time had he wasted resenting her not being Mrs. Shortwell and not being sixty years old. If he had known then what he knew now, that she was going to mean so much to him, he would have welcomed her with open arms.

On the other hand, his open arms might have frightened her off. He watched her sip her soup and nibble on some toast.

"What did you think of me when you first got here?" he asked abruptly.

She set her spoon down and rubbed her forehead. "You seemed brusque and businesslike. I realized you were disappointed, but you didn't hide it very well."

He nodded. "I was obnoxious. Go ahead and say it."

"You were obnoxious then."

He frowned. He hadn't expected her to be so brutally honest.

"I'm sorry. I'm going to make it up to you."

She yawned and gave him a lazy smile that made his heart turn over. He picked up her tray.

"Time for your nap," he told her, the tenderness he felt swelling up around his heart.

She closed her eyes obediently and before he'd left the room she was asleep. Just when he was about to tell her how he felt about her and how he wanted to take care of her forever.

The afternoon dragged by. He looked in at her but she was always asleep, each time in a different position, her dark, glossy hair flung over one cheek or sprayed across the pillow.

He called the doctor again and then Elliott came home from school. He went outside to feed the fish, and Garrett went back upstairs. While he was standing in the doorway watching her sleep she coughed and woke herself up. She looked at him.

"What time is it? I have to make dinner."

He shook his head. "I made it." He sat on her bed again. "The doctor wants to know if you have rales and ronchi."

"What's that?"

"It's a rattling sound in your lungs. Somebody has to listen to your chest." Garrett tried to sound detached, like a kindly, old family practitioner. "Because rales and ronchi are a symptom of pneumonia."

"I thought he didn't make house calls."

"He doesn't, but I do. I wouldn't do it if he hadn't suggested it." His voice sounded normal to his ears, but his heart thudded. He took her hand. "It's all in the interest of science. If he were here you'd let him do it, and you don't even know him."

He thought he saw a glimmer of interest in the corner of Maggie's eyes. "How do you know what to do? You don't have a stethoscope, do you?"

"I don't need one." He tried to keep his eyes off the buttons on her nightgown, off of the pale pink flowers on the flannel that cascaded down over her breasts. She looked so soft, so warm and so utterly desirable. He closed his eyes for a minute in an effort to reestablish his bedside manner. "Rales and ronchi can be heard with the naked ear."

Her eyebrows shot up in alarm.

"Just my ear is naked," he assured her. "You can keep your nightgown on, if you want."

Maggie pulled herself up into a half-sitting position and leaned against her pillow. "I want."

He nodded, keeping his face a mask of professionalism.

"Can you hear all right from there?" Her face was flushed and her eyes had a definite sparkle. Either she was having a good time or she was having a relapse.

"No, I'll have to come a little closer. Just close your eyes and relax."

Miraculously she did as he said. No more questions, no more banter. She just closed her eyes. Her lashes were dark against her pink cheeks. She breathed deeply, the rise and fall of her breasts caused his heart to pound so loudly he wondered how he'd be able to hear anything else. He put his ear against her ribs, his cheek cushioned against the rising swell of her breast. The racing of her heart matched his own. The sound of her heartbeat filled his head, and despite his good intentions he put his arms around her.

"Oh, Maggie," he breathed.

He felt her hands in his hair. The electricity flowed from his body to hers and back again forming an unbreakable circuit. He brought one hand from around her waist to cup her breast.

She took a sharp breath and he turned his head. Instead of his ear against her ribs, his mouth was against the flannel that covered her swelling breast. He reached for the small buttons under the collar of the nightgown.

"Garrett..." Her voice was hoarse. Her hands cradled the back of his head. "I might be contagious."

He looked up at her face. Her head was back on the pillow, her breathing was ragged. Had she fainted, or did she feel the same way he did? On a runaway train, out of control and speeding toward their destiny.

"I have a very strong immune system," he assured her in a low voice.

He felt her arms around his shoulders, and he felt hope surge through his body. If she could act like this when she was sick... He caught himself. He had to remember that she was still sick.

With fumbling fingers he buttoned her nightgown.

Maggie opened her eyes slowly and looked at him. She felt his fingers burn right through the nightgown. She wanted him to stop buttoning it up. She wanted him to pull if off over her head so she could feel his face against her skin. Her whole body ached with desire. Why had he stopped? Didn't he know she never wanted him to stop?

"Garrett, please..."

"I'm sorry. I'm afraid you'll think I planned that." His voice was deep and unsteady. He buttoned the last button and pulled the blanket up to her chin and held it there.

Maggie felt the steady warmth of his hand through the blanket and it seemed to hold the chills at bay. "What did you hear, anyway?" she asked.

"Bells and whistles and firecrackers," he confessed.

She smiled. "Me, too," she whispered.

There was a long silence, and her gaze held his.

"Oh." He seemed to come back to earth with a thud. "You mean what did I hear in your chest. Well..."

"What is it? Go ahead, I can take it."

"Your lungs are clear, it's your heart I'm worried about."

Her head seemed to be floating above her body. She had the strange sensation of being above the bed and looking down at herself. She saw Garrett too, his dark head bent over hers.

"What do you mean?" she heard herself ask. "Is it something like a heart murmur?"

He shook his head. "Not a murmur. It was too loud for that. It was more of a shout. And it was telling me what I wanted to hear." Garrett's eyes smoldered with intensity and Maggie watched, unable to move even a finger. "It was telling me you'll never leave, Maggie, no matter which way the wind blows. You belong to us. That was your heart talking, Maggie. I heard it."

She tried to raise her head, but it felt too heavy. He was taking advantage of her, reading her mind without telling her what was in his. Elliott's footsteps sounded on the stairs and he arrived breathless at her door. Garrett turned in surprise. He'd been so intent he hadn't even heard him coming.

"It's a lady. A lady's at the door asking for Maggie." His blue eyes were wide behind his glasses. "She talks kind of funny."

Maggie sat up, her arms stiff at her sides.

Garrett stood and looked out the window. "There's a big black Cadillac out in front." Two creases formed between his eyebrows. "Who do we know with a Cadillac?"

Maggie groaned and closed her eyes. "Mrs. Newcastle," she murmured. "It must be her. I forgot. It's her annual visit. Is this the eleventh already? How long have I been sick?"

"Mrs. Newcastle? From the nanny agency? What's she doing here?"

Maggie rubbed her fingers across her forehead trying to make the thoughts come forward. It was all too much. Garrett wanted her to stay and Mrs. Newcastle was at the door. Her head throbbed and her pulse raced and her face was on fire.

She licked her dry lips. "I told you she makes an annual visit to all the new graduates to see how they're doing. She interviews the employer and the nanny, then if there's any problem—" Maggie coughed until tears smarted at her eyes. Mrs. Newcastle would see right away there was something going on between her and Garrett. "I'm sure I told you she was coming. You just forgot."

Garrett stared out the window at the Cadillac as if he could make it disappear. "How long will she stay?" he muttered.

Maggie closed her eyes. "Just long enough for the interviews. Not longer than a day."

"A whole day?" Garrett shouted and Maggie's eyes flew open in alarm.

Garrett looked at Elliott. "Go down and tell the lady to come in and sit down. I'll be right there."

Elliott shot out of the room and down the stairs.

Maggie threw back her blankets and lowered her feet to the floor. Garrett crossed the room in two steps and lifted her legs back onto the bed. He threw the blanket back over her and held her down with his hands on her shoulders.

"Stay right where you are. I'll explain to Mrs. Newcastle that you've been sick and that you can't see her."

Maggie shook her head. He didn't know that Mrs. Newcastle had worked her way up from the lower East End of London to the director of a fashionable worldwide nanny service and she hadn't done it by taking no for an answer. She watched Garrett leave the room and she strained to hear their conversation downstairs. She could only hear the rise and fall of their voices and soon Maggie drifted away on the tide of their words.

Chapter Nine

When Maggie woke up it was getting dark outside and she was hungry. Her mouth was dry and her throat hurt. She watched the door, willing it to open and finally it did. An unforgettable scent wafted into the room.

"Hello, dear, are you awake?" Mrs. Newcastle's professionally cheery voice caused Maggie to sit up straight and switch on her bedside lamp.

Mrs. Newcastle, with her perfectly made-up face under a wide-brimmed felt hat, looked out of place on the farm.

Her high heels clicked across the oak floorboards. Without a moment's hesitation she lifted a chair from the corner of the room and placed it next to Maggie's bed. She smoothed her skirt before she sat down.

"How are you?" she inquired. Maggie could see tiny worry lines etched between her eyebrows.

"I'm fine, really," Maggie assured her. She hoped to give the impression that not only was she not very sick, but that she was fine in general, despite appearances to the contrary. She could only guess at what Garrett had told her.

"Hmm." Mrs. Newcastle leaned forward and frowned. "I had no idea it would be like this, Margaret."

"Like what?" Maggie asked. She knew the house was old and that the stairs creaked and slanted to one side. She knew Garrett's jeans had holes in the knees and his shoes were run-down at the heels, but she'd gotten used to these things.

The house was only temporary, and as for Garrett, he was very real and very permanent. No matter what kind of house he lived in he'd be the same—honest, well-worn and unpretentious. And she loved him that way. She felt a surge of protectiveness, as if he needed her protection.

Mrs. Newcastle crossed one knee over the other. "Margaret, this place is a million miles from nowhere. On a dirt road."

"I know. I like it. It's peaceful. And it's not that far from civilization. San Francisco is only a few miles away."

"Oh? How often have you been there since you arrived here?" Mrs. Newcastle held out her hand to prevent her from speaking. "There's no need to answer. Mr. Townsend has already told me that you've scarcely had any days off to go anywhere."

"That's not true," Maggie protested. "We've been to Carmel and Oregon."

But Mrs. Newcastle shook her head sadly as if Maggie had taken a tour of the sewers and visited Alcatraz Island.

"Dinnertime." Elliott's voice rose from the kitchen below, and Maggie's stomach growled. She wanted to get away from Mrs. Newcastle's disapproving eyes and into the warm, bright kitchen where something smelled very good.

"You'll stay for dinner, won't you?" Maggie asked, testing her wobbly legs by standing next to her bed.

"Of course. Mr. Townsend was kind enough to invite me and I haven't had a chance to talk to you yet."

Maggie's knees buckled and Mrs. Newcastle put her arm around her waist and helped her into her bathrobe.

"But the little boy has been very cooperative," she continued. "He told me quite a bit about your life here." Mrs. Newcastle walked Maggie to the door and down the stairs.

"Oh." Mrs. Newcastle had apparently already spoken to both Garrett and Elliott and heaven only knew what they'd told her.

Maggie's nose quivered at the smell of a pot roast simmering on top of the gas range, and she felt a rush of warmth as if she had suddenly come in out of a storm.

"Maggie!" Elliott jumped off of his stool at the kitchen counter and hugged her around the knees. He'd never made such a display of affection before and Maggie was so touched tears sprang to her eyes. After all those hours in bed her knees seemed to be made of rubber and she sank gratefully into one of the kitchen chairs.

Garrett turned and looked her over. "Not so hard, Elliott. Maggie has to be handled gently." His eyes gleamed his approval at seeing her up. "Don't you agree, Mrs. Newcastle?"

Mrs. Newcastle looked from Garrett to Maggie, then sat down at the end of the table. "I certainly do. If she'd been treated gently, she might not have gotten sick."

"But Mrs. Newcastle," Maggie said, "you're the one who taught me about the germ theory. I didn't get sick from jumping in the water. I have an upper respiratory infection I caught from somebody."

Mrs. Newcastle frowned. "Jumping in what water?"

"Maggie jumped in the pond to catch Big Lou," Elliott explained.

Maggie smiled. "No, I didn't, Elliott. I jumped in to get that little girl who caught Big Lou."

Mrs. Newcastle's lips pursed together. "I hope Big Lou fared better than Maggie. Whoever he is, I assume he doesn't work on Sundays, and neither do our nannies, Mr. Townsend."

Garrett set the pot roast on a platter, surrounded it with small boiled potatoes and carrots and covered it with a thick, brown gravy.

"I thought Maggie would enjoy a day outside fishing in the fresh air and sunshine," Garrett said nonchalantly. He placed the steaming platter in the middle of the table and took his place in the high-backed chair at the end of the table. "But fishing is like life—you never know what's going to happen next. And Maggie turned out to be the heroine of the day."

"Maggie weighs the fish and I bait the hooks," Elliott explained proudly.

"I'm delighted to hear it." Mrs. Newcastle cut her meat in small, neat pieces. "What I'm wondering is how Maggie will be compensated for spending her days off jumping into ponds to rescue people who shouldn't be there in the first place."

"I've been wondering that myself." Garrett gazed thoughtfully at Maggie.

"It could be done with compensatory time off or in salary," Mrs. Newcastle suggested, spearing a carrot on her plate.

"We'll be going skiing at Christmas," Garrett offered, "but I suppose you wouldn't count that."

Maggie set her fork down in surprise. Garrett had never mentioned skiing. Here we go again, she thought. Another surprise vacation.

"If you mean you're taking Maggie along as a nanny, you certainly couldn't count that."

"I'm taking Maggie along because I can't get along without her," Garrett announced firmly.

Mrs. Newcastle smiled with satisfaction. "I'm happy to say that most all of our employers feel just as you do about our girls."

"Do they?" Garrett asked raising his eyebrows in surprise. Maggie heard him mutter something under his breath that sounded like, "They ought to be locked up."

Maggie felt his hand on her knee under the table and she suddenly felt so light-headed and giddy that she giggled. She covered her mouth and coughed.

"Where do you ski?" Mrs. Newcastle asked in an effort to bring the conversation back to normal.

"We have a cabin at Tahoe." Garrett found Maggie's hand on her lap and squeezed it gently.

"Ah..." Mrs. Newcastle said looking around the kitchen. "Roughing it."

"Not exactly." Garrett signaled to Elliott to clear the table. "It has a hot tub and a nice view of the lake."

"Do you know the Halvorsons? They spend the holidays at the lake, too."

Garrett shook his head. "I don't think so."

"They have a new baby and they're looking for a nanny." Mrs. Newcastle looked at Maggie. "Good nannies are very hard to find."

Maggie felt Garrett's eyes on her.

"We're very grateful to you for sending Maggie to us," he said solemnly.

"That was a mistake."

"I don't think so. I think it was fate."

Mrs. Newcastle snorted a ladylike snort.

Garrett put his elbows on the table and leaned forward. "Don't you believe in fate, Mrs. Newcastle? I do. I even believe in fortune-tellers. I had one tell me I was going to get married again and have more children. So you see, I'll need Maggie more than ever."

Maggie's face felt hot and her heart skipped a beat. She knew she should go back to bed, but she didn't want to miss any of this conversation. She could hear the hum of the television set in the living room. Elliott hadn't found the conversation interesting enough to compete with the Monday-night football game.

"People like the Halvorsons have a great deal to offer a nanny, besides fresh air and sunshine. Maggie needs to meet people, the right kind of people. The Halvorsons have a very active social life." Mrs. Newcastle looked pointedly at Garrett.

"So do I," he insisted. "Just the other day I had lunch with the best well-digger in Stanislaus County. Maggie met him, too, didn't you? Oh, no, that was the surveyor. Well, anyway—" he gestured expansively at Mrs. Newcastle and smiled engagingly "—you get the picture."

Mrs. Newcastle stood up and pushed her chair in. "I'm afraid I do get the picture, only too clearly. And whatever parts of the picture I haven't gotten, I will get after I speak to Maggie." She put her arms around Maggie and pulled her to her feet. "My girls come first with me, Mr. Townsend."

Maggie gave a helpless backward look at Garrett as Mrs. Newcastle led her up the stairs.

Maggie sat up in her bed feeling apprehensive as Mrs. Newcastle took out a yellow legal tablet and a pencil and sat in the chair next to her bed. She didn't want to answer any questions until she knew what Garrett and Elliott had said, but she couldn't admit that.

Mrs. Newcastle held her pencil poised above the paper and frowned at Maggie. "I'm very disappointed to find you like this, Margaret."

"You mean my being sick," suggested Maggie. "I should have called you and postponed your visit."

"You wouldn't have found me in the office. I was in Carmel visiting Doreen Carmichael. Such a lovely situation." Her eyes darted around Maggie's room, taking in the faded wallpaper and the plain, unvarnished dresser.

Maggie followed her gaze. "This is just temporary," she explained.

"Indeed it is. If I had known the nature of this Mr. Townsend and his trout farm, I would never have let one of my girls come." She leaned forward. "Mr. Townsend seems to care about you Maggie, in his own rough-hewn way, and I can see that he does have a certain rustic charm. Has he ever made any advances toward you?"

Maggie's eyes widened in mock horror. "Oh, no," she assured Mrs. Newcastle. "He's been a perfect gentleman. He has a great respect for our profession, actually."

"Really." Mrs. Newcastle leaned back in her chair, slightly mollified. "Originally Mr. Townsend requested an older woman, and because of the mistake at our end I feel morally obliged to provide him with one."

"I think he's changed his mind," Maggie suggested hastily, "or did he...did he ask you to replace me?" Maggie suddenly felt the chills coming back at the thought of leaving Garrett. How could she bear to leave him, but how could she bear to stay when she couldn't give him what he wanted.

"No, no, of course not. He indicated that he's completely satisfied with your work. And it's natural for my clients to become attached to their nannies and the nannies to the families. That's why I'm here, to sift through the emotionalism and do what's best for all parties. I know what you're going to say, Margaret, but do let me remind you that I've had years of experience in this sort of thing. And all I'm suggesting is that you meet with the Halvorsons. Perhaps at Lake Tahoe at Christmas vacation when it would be convenient for all of you. Mr. Townsend has given me the address of his cabin up there."

So Garrett had given Mrs. Newcastle the address. Maybe he wasn't as opposed to Maggie's leaving as she had thought he'd be. Suddenly she was exhausted.

"All right, fine."

Mrs. Newcastle smiled with satisfaction and stood up. "Before I leave, I must say that you've done an exemplary job here, considering what you had to work with. I don't know anyone else who would have stuck it out." The lines around her mouth relaxed. "The little boy is quite well-behaved, and he seems very fond of you."

Maggie smiled. "I'm fond of him, too." She bit her lip. The implication was that Garrett was not well-behaved and was not fond of Maggie. Was that what she meant?

Mrs. Newcastle looked at her watch. "I must be off. I have a reservation at the Half Moon Bay bed-and-breakfast inn tonight and an appointment to see a family there tomorrow. A lovely home on the golf course right on the fourth fairway." She looked out the window at the dark bare hills and Maggie knew she was thinking they couldn't compare to manicured green lawn. Mrs. Newcastle blew her a kiss from the doorway.

"Keep an open mind, Margaret, and get well soon. I'll be thinking of you."

After Mrs. Newcastle had left and Garrett had put Elliott to bed, Garrett paced around the house feeling like a caged tiger. He turned on the television and snapped it off. He picked up an old magazine and set it down. Of all times for the woman to come. She'd caught Maggie feeling weak and sick and promised her a life in the lap of luxury. A life he couldn't offer her, and wouldn't if he could.

A fancy house. Beautiful children with expensive clothes. Meeting the right people. Was that what Maggie wanted? He heard her voice calling him and he rushed up the stairs.

"Garrett," she called hoarsely.

He opened her door. In the light from the hall he saw her lying on her side, her eyes closed, her blankets in a heap at her feet. He walked softly across the room and sat on the edge of her bed. She was sound asleep. He stroked her forehead, lifting the soft brown hair back from her face.

"What is it, Maggie?" he asked softly, but she didn't answer. He pulled a blanket from the end of the bed and covered her.

There were tiny beads of perspiration on her forehead and he stood to get a towel to wipe them off. In the bathroom that she shared with Elliott he soaked a washcloth in cold water and squeezed it dry.

"Don't leave," she muttered.

He patted her forehead gently. "I'm not leaving," he promised.

"I can't help it," Maggie said. "I love him, Mrs. Newcastle."

"What?" Garrett's heart pounded and Maggie opened her eyes and looked at him with the vacant stare of a sleepwalker.

She gripped his arms. "But what about the baby?" she demanded in a choked voice and a tear ran down her cheek.

Garrett leaned over. "Don't worry about the baby. We'll have our own baby." Garrett's voice sounded just as choked as Maggie's. He put his cheek next to hers and she felt as if she was burning up. She continued to mumble but he couldn't make any sense out of it, except that she wanted a baby. That much was clear. Well, dammit, he'd give her a baby.

He dragged the chair next to her bed and watched her restless sleep. The doctor had said to expect chills and fever and he wanted to be there when the chills came to make sure she was warm enough.

When they finally came her body felt cold and clammy to the touch and he held her against him to transfer some of his body heat to her. She shivered and he brought a quilt from the closet to cover her. He thought she smiled at him, but she might have been dreaming. After a while he didn't know if he was awake or dreaming himself. When she finally fell into a normal sleep, he staggered downstairs to his own room and fell asleep with his clothes on.

Maggie woke up feeling the weight of the extra blankets and the quilt. She lay there feeling almost normal except for the dry, scratchy throat and the headache. Had Mrs. Newcastle been there or had she dreamed it? Whose gentle hands had soothed her in the night?

She squinted at the small clock on her bedside table. It was after nine and the house was quiet again. She had to see who was there and what was happening. She had to be sure Elliott had gone to school and Garrett had gone back to work at the river and Mrs. Newcastle was safely on the fourth fairway of the golf course in Half Moon Bay.

Without bothering to put on a bathrobe, she tiptoed barefoot down the stairs. On the kitchen table was a bowl with a few grains of cereal left in it. Elliott's backpack was gone from the hook by the door. She looked out the front window and saw only one car, Garrett's. But where was he? She walked to the end of the hallway and listened at his bedroom door. She leaned against it and the door swung open. Garrett lay sound asleep facedown on top of the bed, completely dressed in the same clothes he had been wearing last night. She wanted to wake him up by running her hand through his dark, shaggy hair.

The door creaked and Garrett turned over and opened his eyes. His eyelids were heavy and his face was unshaven. He held out his arms for her, but Maggie flattened her back against the wall. The shadow of Mrs. Newcastle hung over the house. She suddenly saw herself as Mrs. Newcastle might see her, in her nightgown in her employer's bedroom. She shuddered at the idea of being caught there.

Garrett stretched and yawned, pretending he didn't want her so badly it hurt like a toothache, nagging and insistent.

"I was wondering where you were," she explained.

"I'm in bed where you're supposed to be." He stood up slowly and walked over to her and gently pinned her to the wall with his arms. "You know what I mean."

"I dreamed about you last night."

He pulled her toward him, his hands under her elbows, and touched her forehead against his. Her face blurred and she closed her eyes. He supported her with his weight and his warmth.

"You did? Tell me about it."

"I don't remember very well. But I was hot and somebody with cool hands held me."

Garrett put his arm around her shoulders and led her down the hall. "That wasn't a dream, that was real."

They walked up the narrow staircase together, Garrett's hip pressed against hers, his arm around her waist. At the doorway she paused and looked at her bed, the wrinkled sheets, the blankets at the foot of the bed. She glanced at Garrett and their eyes held and locked.

She saw naked desire reflected there and it shocked her. Suddenly she felt hollow and unfulfilled. If she weren't sick, she knew no nanny rule book would stop her from going to bed with Garrett. She ached with desire, and she ached with the flu and together the ache became a throbbing need.

"Get into bed," Garrett ordered gruffly. "I'll make you some breakfast." But before he made the breakfast, he made a telephone call to his real-estate agent and told him to make an offer on the property that wouldn't be refused—the full asking price. He was relieved, he was excited. He was also scared out of his wits.

When he returned to Maggie's room with her hot cereal and orange juice on a tray, he had his emotions under control. This was not the time to tell her he'd bought the property for her, for them, for their life together. Christmas was the time, he decided with unexplainable certainty. Her first Christmas with them but not the last, if he had anything to say about it.

"Feeling better?"

Maggie nodded, afraid to trust her voice. What was going to happen to them when she got well, she didn't dare think about.

Fortunately, very fortunately, Maggie told herself, things went back to normal when she got well. Garrett went back to the river with renewed enthusiasm after giving her an absentminded kiss. Elliott went off to school in the mornings. Maggie made cookies and popcorn and hot chocolate for him when he came home. She didn't think about the future.

She started knitting Garrett's Christmas sweater with the sea-green yarn she'd bought before Thanksgiving. She found it soothing to knit in the evenings after Elliott had gone to bed. And she could picture Garrett wearing the sweater skiing.

It was only two weeks until Christmas, and she kept waiting for him to bring up the subject of the ski vacation, but all he could talk about when he came home on the weekend was the land he'd bought. He was more excited about having his offer accepted than she'd imagined. He had ordered the cement mixer to pour the concrete for the foundation of the house, but he was worried it would rain before they came. This obsession with the next phase of his life made her feel left out. Had their vacation slipped his mind?

"Garrett," she interrupted one evening as he was talking about rights-of-way and escrow, "it's been a long time since I've been skiing, and I don't know—"

"That's all right," he assured her. "I'll ski with you while Elliott's having his lessons." He paused. "I don't know what I want. I want it to snow in the mountains, but if it snows up there it will probably rain on my foundation. Do you see my problem?"

He grabbed her around the waist and lifted her in the air with a quizzical grin on his face, then set her down and went out the back door to the pond. She stood staring at his back, her mouth open with surprise. Would she ever understand him? She picked up the sweater from under the cushion on the couch and knitted automatically. How long should she make the sleeves. How long?

The words went round and round in her head. How long would she be here with them? How long would it take to build the house? Yes, she saw his problem, but it was nothing compared to hers. Her days were numbered, and she cherished every one.

Chapter Ten

There was no rain until the concrete had set, then it came down in sheets. The same gray clouds dumped heaps of snow around Lake Tahoe. Maggie wasn't surprised to see the elements cooperate with Garrett. They knew when they'd met their match. Maggie wondered if she'd met hers, too.

Garrett came home only the night before they left for the mountains so Maggie could pack up the car with skis and Christmas presents. She'd made a wooden brontosaurus for Elliott out of a kit and had painted it brown while he slept at night. She'd bought him a Swiss Army knife and books she could read to him.

Fortunately Garrett and Elliott's skis went on a rack on top of the car, because Maggie's presents filled the trunk and overflowed into the backseat.

"What is all this stuff?" Garrett asked, as he wedged his ski parka into a small space in the trunk.

Elliott's eyes glowed. There were boxes next to him and boxes on the floor in front of him.

"Christmas presents," he said gleefully. Maggie knew that he'd made something for Garrett at school and that he'd carefully placed it at the bottom of his duffel bag under his clothes.

Garrett closed the trunk and looked over the top of the car at Maggie. Lines creased his broad forehead. "There aren't any presents for me, are there? I mean you didn't...I didn't." He stared distractedly at Maggie and ran his hand through his hair.

Maggie smiled to herself. She had caught Garrett off guard and she was one up on him. "Of course not," she assured him. "It wouldn't be appropriate for us to exchange presents. After all, you're my employer and I'm your son's nanny." She knew she sounded prim, but she couldn't help it. She didn't want Garrett to give her anything impersonal like a box of candy. She'd rather have nothing at all, and it looked as if that was what she was going to get.

Garrett leaned against the car and looked at Maggie. She noticed the elbow of his sweater was wearing thin and she thought about the sweater in a box in the backseat. She'd made a few mistakes, but she hoped he wouldn't notice.

"You don't have to remind me who you are," he said. "But there must be something that's appropriate. Why don't you look in your nanny's handbook?"

"I have. You could give me stationery or a calendar."

He shook his head. "I want to give you something meaningful...like a new nightgown."

"Garrett." Maggie glared at him and looked pointedly at Elliott who was sitting in the backseat looking at a comic book.

He grinned. "I'm just kidding. I know I can't do that. Besides I like the one you have now, the soft one with the little flowers on it."

Maggie flushed. She hadn't packed that nightgown. Instead, for some reason, she had brought one she'd never worn before, pale green silk with lace at the top. Totally wrong for a ski cabin, but Maggie could always resort to her long underwear if it was cold in the bedroom.

"Christmas is for children," she announced righteously. "You and I don't need any presents."

"You're right, as usual," Garrett agreed, pulling out of the driveway.

"Just like Mary Poppins," Elliott said from the back-seat. "Did Mary Poppins know how to ski, anyway, Maggie?"

"Yes she did," Maggie answered quickly, grateful to him for changing the subject.

Elliott paused, his lips parted, waiting to hear more.

"Is there anything that woman can't do?" Garrett asked.

"Mary Poppins? Well, let me see . . ." She couldn't have children of her own, Maggie thought, a tight knot forming in her stomach. That was the only thing she couldn't do, and that was the most important thing of all.

Garrett drove with his eyes on the road but his mind on Maggie. It was so easy for him to imagine the three of them as a family. Could Maggie imagine it, too? He hadn't said anything to her since the day she had gotten sick, but from that moment on, when he'd seen her there in bed, needing him, he was determined to make her part of his life.

His offer on the property was immediately snapped up and everything clicked into place. His dream of a property and his dream of a woman. It was all possible. It just took persistence and some luck. If this vacation went the way he thought it would—soft lights and mistletoe and music and laughter and presents . . .

What could he give her for a present? Something personal like a black negligee would embarrass her and something impersonal like a magazine subscription wouldn't mean anything. The picture of Maggie wearing a black negligee was a tantalizing one. He turned toward her and with his eyes he peeled away the turtleneck and the blue-and-white ski sweater and imagined her with the black straps over her shoulders, her dark hair brushing against his face as she thanked him for his present.

She turned and met his gaze. She opened her mouth to speak and closed it again. Her face reddened. "Don't look at me like that."

"Sorry. I didn't know you read minds, too."

She looked out the side window. "Oh, yes, I'm a compulsive reader."

"I have a few compulsions myself," he admitted softly, and he glanced at the back of her head, still turned to the window. Garrett was counting on this vacation, this change of scene to bring about the change in their relationship. Getting her out of the house where their roles were well defined was the first step.

The second step was to convince her that she ought to marry him. She had to marry him. He knew what she'd say. She'd said it all before. That she wasn't good at marriage. She'd failed once. Well, he'd failed once, too. That didn't mean that they didn't deserve a second chance. He was counting on the cabin and the hot tub on the deck and the master bedroom with the view of the lake to work their magic.

If that didn't work, he didn't know what he'd do. He gripped the steering wheel so tightly his knuckles were white. He couldn't live with her in that farmhouse anymore and maintain his sanity. He couldn't sleep downstairs in his bedroom knowing she was just upstairs in her bed. He wanted her so badly he couldn't stop thinking about her, at the river where he was pouring concrete or driving back home at breakneck speed to see her on the weekend.

He thought she'd agree if he put it the right way, but he'd been wrong about Maggie before. He couldn't be sure of anything. His throat was too dry to speak. The anxiety was getting to him.

The cabin didn't let him down. She stood in the middle of the sunken living room and looked around while he built a fire in the huge fireplace.

"You said a cabin," she murmured, her eyes taking in the balcony with the skylight above it and the large, comfortable armchairs on either side of the massive stone fireplace.

"It's nice, isn't it? I bought it as an investment when I sold the salmon trawler. I rent it out most of the season, but never at Christmas. Christmas is our time." He stressed the "our" to include her, and she noticed—she must have noticed. Or was it just wishful thinking?

Elliott found his sled in the storage closet and went outside on the hill next to the house.

Garrett took Maggie on a tour of the house, ending with the master bedroom down the hall from the living room. Framed in the window, the lake sparkled in the bright cold sunlight with the dazzling white mountains behind it.

Maggie took a deep breath. "It's beautiful."

Garrett reached down to switch on the heat in the king-size water bed. "I thought you'd like it."

"Like it?" She stared as if mesmerized by the scene. "Yes, I like it. Imagine looking out at this when you wake up in the morning."

"Uh-huh, but don't lie here too long, we want to be on the slopes when the lifts open."

"Wait a minute." She shifted her gaze from the view to his face. "This is your room, isn't it?"

He shook his head. "Not this time. I'll take one of the small bedrooms in the loft."

"How come?" Her eyes narrowed.

"How come? I'm trying to impress you." He reached down to test the bed. It undulated softly, ripples moving from his side to hers and she looked down as if she hadn't seen it before.

"It's so big," she murmured. She looked at Garrett and wondered who had slept with him here before. Not Helena, because he bought the cabin with the money from the sale of the trawler after the end of their marriage. Did he expect her to sleep with him there? His face gave no hint of any such expectation. In fact, the lines deepening between his eyebrows made him look anxious.

"I am impressed," she assured him.

Maggie was even more impressed when they went out to cut down a Christmas tree from Garrett's own property.

"Elliott has had one picked out since last year." Garrett pointed to a twelve-foot-tall ponderosa pine at the rear of the property.

"But you can't do this every year," Maggie protested. "You won't have any trees left on the property."

"We replant in the spring," he assured her. "They grow like weeds." He looked at the tree critically. "It's a little thin on this side, though." He pulled Maggie by the arm so she could examine it from all sides.

She looked up at the dark green branches, inhaled the fresh pine smell and nodded her approval. The cold air on her face and the warmth of Garrett's hand on her arm made her blood race in exhilaration. To be in love at Christmas could be ecstatic or miserable. The season heightened every feeling. And right now Maggie was ecstatic.

Garrett handed her one end of a handsaw and she plopped down in the soft snow and pulled the blade across the trunk of the tree while Garrett pushed. Then he pulled while she pushed and the saw formed a bond between them. The sap oozed onto Maggie's glove and the pungent smell that it released filled her with a longing for every Christmas to be this perfect.

When the tree began to wobble, Maggie leaped up and watched Garrett catch it. Elliott clapped his approval and helped his father carry it into the living room.

The tree almost touched the top of the vaulted ceiling and looked as if it belonged there. After dinner Maggie popped corn to string with cranberries. She pictured an old-fashioned tree with only homemade decorations. But Elliott and Garrett ate the corn as fast as she popped it, and Elliott begged for the cranberries to feed the squirrels. Maggie was too tired to protest. She'd start all over the next night, and she'd set Elliott to work making paper chains while she handled the edible decorations herself.

Elliott told Maggie to leave the room while he put her present under the tree, and Maggie seized the opportunity to say good-night to both of them and escape to the luxurious bedroom suite.

After a soak in the deep porcelain tub with the claw feet, Maggie took out the long silk nightgown that she'd bought months ago, before she'd ever heard of Garrett Townsend and his son and his trout farm. She hastily pulled the pale green gown over her head and slid under the fluffy quilt onto undulating waves of water. Did she really want Garrett to see her in this nightgown?

There was a knock on the door, and startled, Maggie pulled the quilt up to her chin.

"Maggie, it's me. Can I come in?" Garrett asked.

Maggie had a sudden attack of cold feet. Her feet felt like ice. She shivered. No matter what happened, Garrett must never know what she was wearing. She imagined what he'd think if he saw her. All the public relations about nannies she'd been doing ever since her arrival would go down the drain.

"Come in."

"It's about time." He stepped in quietly and his eyes roamed over the outline of her body under the quilt. "I thought you'd gotten seasick from the waves." He reached over to press down on the mattress.

She shook her head.

"You're shivering. It isn't warm enough. I'll turn the heat up."

Maggie leaned over to hold the setting where it was, losing her grip on the quilt. Too late she remembered the see-through bodice.

Garrett stopped, bent over her bed, his hand reaching for the control. His eyes were fastened on the nightgown. Maggie stared back at him; his thick fisherman's sweater emphasized his shoulders, his broad chest. She imagined the feel of the soft wool against the silk of her nightgown.

Garrett straightened slowly. "No wonder you're cold. You can't wear something like that in the mountains." His voice was rough and uneven.

With one swift motion Maggie slid back under the quilt. "It's warm, honestly," she said realizing she was babbling but unable to stop. "If you were in here you'd see, but you're not, I mean, not tonight."

Garrett walked across the room and stood by the window. The moon shone on the mountains with a clear white brilliance. He couldn't have planned a more impressive show for Maggie.

She followed his gaze. "It's a beautiful sight. I'll bet you wish you were sleeping here." She blushed. "I mean because of the view."

He stared out the window, afraid to look at her. "Yes, I do," he said in a strangled voice. If he turned around, he didn't know how he could stay away from her. Why had she worn that nightgown? He felt torn up inside. He turned and sat down in the large, polished oak rocker in the corner and gripped the smooth, rounded arms with his wide fingers. He was desperate. This called for shock tactics. His eyes smoldered and burned bright enough to sear through the quilt and the nightgown.

"Maggie," Garrett made a superhuman effort to keep his voice steady, "you're fired."

She sat up again, the lace pulled to one side to expose her pale skin. "What?"

He swallowed hard. "You heard me."

Her eyes blazed back at him. "You can't fire me. I haven't done anything wrong."

"Haven't done anything wrong? You lost Big Lou, you've misrepresented Mary Poppins by putting her in a time frame with dinosaurs, you got me in trouble with Mrs. Newcastle by not taking your days off. And that's not all."

Maggie's eyes were round, her lips were parted in surprise and bright spots of color were on her cheeks. Now that Garrett had started, he knew he had to finish.

"That's not all, that's just the beginning. The worst of it is that I'm not happy with my life anymore."

Maggie bit her bottom lip, and Garrett had to force himself to stay where he was. Every fiber of his being wanted to cross the room and kiss her lips, her cheeks and her eyes.

"That's not my fault," she protested.

"Yes it is. You've made me want things I can't have, at least not with a nanny in the house."

Maggie forced her lips to move. "You want to get married again and have more children."

He nodded. "Before you came I was happy with what I had. One child and a house and my pond. Now I see the possibilities for more." He hesitated and studied her face; her bright eyes focused on him. "Don't you?" he added softly.

"Oh yes, I don't blame you." She pulled back the quilt and sat on the edge of the bed. "When do you want me to leave?" Maggie's silk nightgown clung to her curves. Her chin was set at such a determined angle Garrett almost thought she might walk out right then and there into the snow.

"I don't want you to leave." He stood up and clenched his fists. "I want you to marry me."

The color drained from her face and tears glazed her eyes. Then her chin fell forward and all he could see was the top of her head.

Garrett's heart fell with a thud. He didn't know what to expect, but it wasn't this picture of dejection. "Never mind." He crossed the room and held her by the shoulders. "Forget what I said. Forget the whole thing. I'd rather have you for a nanny than lose you."

A tear trickled down her cheek and he bent over and kissed it. "Maggie, please don't do that. I'm sorry. I . . . it was too much of a shock. And I said it all wrong."

She pressed her lips together and shook her head. "It's not that. I think it would be wonderful to be married to you."

"Maggie, please." There was a hollow space in his chest where his heart used to be. "Don't be polite. I can stand anything, but don't tell me what you think I want to hear."

He couldn't stand up anymore. He knelt down on his knees next to her bed until his eyes were on a level with hers. Her face was still pale, but her voice was steady.

"Garrett, I can't get married again, not to you or to anybody. It's not fair, especially for somebody who wants to have more children. I should have told you before, but . . ." Maggie got back under the blankets and pulled her knees up to her chin as if to protect herself. Why hadn't she mentioned it just casually before, her three miscarriages? Was it that she felt ashamed of her failure or did she know, deep down, that once Garrett found out it would be the end of something so fragile she couldn't be sure it existed? She took a deep breath.

"I had three miscarriages while I was married. The first one wasn't so bad—you can always tell yourself it was a fluke. But the second made me wonder, then the third, and I didn't wonder any more. I knew. I just wasn't destined to have children of my own." She stared out the window at the moonlit mountains without seeing them.

Garrett stood up and walked to the end of the bed. "Who said?"

"Nobody said. Nobody had to say. Everybody knew. The doctor, Ted and I. It was the end of our marriage and I blame myself for that. I just wasn't strong enough to hold things together." She shook her head. "I didn't even try." Her voice dipped to a whisper. "I didn't even try."

"And you think that would happen again if you were married to me?" Garrett asked incredulously. His heart ached for Maggie. He didn't wait for an answer. "Well, it wouldn't. First I don't believe that you can't have a baby. There are women who've had seven and eight miscarriages, then go on to have a baby. And if it did happen again to you, there's no way I'd let you get away or suffer by yourself.'' Garrett leaned against the bed.

Maggie's forehead was furrowed and her eyes seemed to plead with him to stop talking about it. He ran his hand through his hair. If only he could get into that bed, hold her and comfort her, he thought he could change her mind. But he could tell from the weariness around her eyes she wasn't ready.

''Don't worry about it,'' he told her from the doorway, and even as he said them the words sounded hollow to his ears. ''We'll work it out.''

She was staring out the window when he left and he didn't even know if she'd heard what he said.

Maggie woke up just as the first rays of sun were coming up over the mountains. She lay perfectly still, as if one movement might prevent the miracle of the sunrise from happening. And how she hoped for a miracle. For herself and for Garrett. Because if there were no miracles and she couldn't have a baby, they had no future together. No matter what he said, she saw the longing in his eyes and she knew what he wanted.

How often had Garrett lain in this same bed watching the sun rise? She ticked off the days before Christmas on her fingers. Was this going to be her first or last Christmas with Garrett? Only nature knew the answer to that, and nature was so fickle.

Maggie could find no fault with nature that day. The snow was deep and powdery; the morning air crisp and the sun shone bright on the blue-white slopes. They dropped Elliott at the ski school, signed him up for morning and afternoon lessons with lunch in between.

Garrett watched Maggie lift herself gracefully out of the chair on the top of the ridge and glide over to join him. Even with his goggles, his head pounded from the glare of the snow and the sleepless night he'd spent. He gestured to the

slope that stretched before them, pure, pristine and un-
touched, and she nodded her agreement. He didn't trust
himself to speak.

They traversed the slopes in perfect synchronization as if
they'd done it all their lives. In spite of the agony of uncertainty Garrett felt his body respond to the harmony of the
wind and the snow and the pure joy of acceleration. At the
bottom he turned to watch Maggie turn her skis sharply to
pull up next to him.

"Margaret Chisholm, you are a fraud, a cheat and a
hustler."

She lifted her sunglasses for a moment to look at him.
"How do you mean?"

"You told me you weren't very good at skiing."

"I said I hadn't skied for a long time. That was true." She
tapped the snow off of her skis.

"That's what you said about Monopoly, too, before you
wiped me out."

A hint of a smile tugged at her lips. Last night he thought
he'd never see her smile again. "You take these things too
seriously," she said. "These are sports and games, that's
all."

"That's all? You'd take them seriously too if you ever
lost. Next time I'll race you down."

They rode the lift together; their skis crossed acciden-
tally and stayed that way. Garrett leaned over and brushed
the snow off of Maggie's jacket. He tried to think of another reason to touch her, but he couldn't.

When they reached the top the sun was so warm that
Maggie took off her jacket and tied it around her waist.
Garrett raised his eyebrows and she nodded. He didn't mean
to give her a head start. She didn't need it, but his boot strap
came loose and when he straightened up she was off like a
shot.

She didn't see the man coming out of nowhere, hotdog-
ging down the hill in a straight line, and he didn't see her
until it was too late and he'd knocked her down and sprayed

her with snow. But Garrett saw the whole thing and pushed off with a burst of speed. By the time he'd reached Maggie she was sitting up, testing her knees.

"The guy was an idiot," he fumed. "How are you?"

"I'm okay, just wet." She pulled at her wet T-shirt, clinging to her body.

He skied with her back to the lodge, and locked their skis together in front of the ski school. Then they walked back to the cabin.

"I want to ski some more," Maggie said, limping slightly.

"After a hot tub and some dry clothes," Garrett promised.

On the deck he lifted the redwood cover of the hot tub for her and left the house noisily and deliberately to split firewood behind the garage. The hot tub was on the deck outside of the master bedroom, but Garrett was aware that there were views of the tub from the deck above or from the bedroom window. And he knew his limitations.

Maggie peeled off her clothes and walked out across the deck on bare feet to the steaming tub. She'd heard Garrett leave the house so she didn't even bother to wear her white terry-cloth robe, which she carried over her arm.

The cold dry air raised goose bumps all over her bare body and she shivered in anticipation of the hot tub. She tested the water with her toe and gently eased herself into the deep, hot water. The heat permeated her body and as she leaned her head back against the side of the tub she felt every tense muscle relax. She looked up at the cloudless sky above and tried to make her mind a blank slate.

She closed her eyes. She would not think about Garrett, although she could hear the sharp blows of his ax against wood somewhere behind the house and she could picture his arms poised over the logs. She'd seen him split wood at home; she knew he used it as a way to release tension as well as for exercise.

She would not think about leaving Garrett, although he had tried to fire her. She was suspended in limbo. She looked around at the pines, heavy with snow. It was a very picturesque limbo, but still a limbo with no way out.

A far-ringing sound found its way to her waterlogged mind. She shook her head and it rang again. She stood up in the tub, waist-deep in water and listened. It could be the front door. It could be Elliott with a broken leg. She thrust her arms through the sleeves of her robe and ran across the deck through the bedroom and into the sunken living room.

The front doorbell was ringing loudly, insistently, and Garrett was still outside at the woodpile. She peered through the peephole in the solid oak front door and saw the face of a baby, magnified and up close. Maggie gasped and wrapped her robe around her tightly. She opened the door, forgetting how she looked. A baby at the front door must be answered.

When the door swung open Maggie saw that the baby was accompanied by a tall, blond woman.

"I'm Mavis Halvorson." The well-groomed, athletic-looking woman extended her free hand toward Maggie and Maggie shook hands with her. "I'm looking for Margaret Chisholm."

Maggie nodded. "I'm Maggie. Won't you come in?" she asked as graciously as she could in her half-dressed state.

Mavis Halvorson looked around the spacious, well-furnished living room with its twelve-foot undecorated tree in the front window and then at Maggie's damp hair and robe.

"Mrs. Newcastle told me it was all right to come, but I should have called first. I'm afraid I'm interrupting something."

Maggie knotted her belt in place and gestured to the couch just as if she were expecting company. "No, not at all. We're . . . I'm just taking a break from skiing. Sit down."

Mrs. Halvorson smiled gratefully and set the baby on the couch. Maggie stared at its tiny fists and scrunched-up face under a pink woolly hat. A fierce longing filled her heart.

Mrs. Halvorson cleared her throat and Maggie looked up. "I guess Mrs. Newcastle told you I'm looking for a nanny. She thought you might be interested in making a change. She says you're one of the best."

Maggie's eyes were riveted to the baby on the couch. "I like babies," she said.

Mrs. Halvorson picked up her baby and set her gently into Maggie's lap. "Her name is Camille," she offered.

Blue eyes looked up at Maggie and tiny fingers closed around her finger. She felt her heart contract as if it, too, were in the hands of this soft, round-faced infant.

Maggie bent her head and touched her forehead against the baby's, inhaling the rare fragrance of babyhood.

"I have three other children. They're all out skiing. Camille will be, too, as soon as she's able to stand up. My husband is big on fitness." Mrs. Halvorson sat up straight and tucked her stomach in.

Maggie lifted the baby out of her lap and looked at her long and hard.

Mrs. Halvorson spoke. "She's sweet, isn't she? But frankly, at this stage of my life she's more than I can handle. I'm desperate for some help."

Maggie nodded. She understood desperation. She was desperate, too, desperate for a baby to hold, to love. All she had to do was to nod her head. She didn't even have to say a word. She could just walk down the hall and get her suitcase and this baby would be hers. This baby wanted her, needed her.

Maggie rested her cheek next to the baby's velvety cheek. Could she do it? Could she walk out on Garrett and Elliott? "You've made me want things I can't have," Garrett had said. Was it fair to him to stay? He wants to get married again and have more children, she told herself, and you're standing in his way. Last night he told her she was fired, and today somebody offered her a job, a job with a baby. It must be fate. Maggie didn't have the strength to fight fate anymore.

She looked up at the tree and at Elliott's present for her under the branches.

She licked her dry lips. "I couldn't leave until after Christmas."

Mrs. Halvorson shrugged and raised her palms. "Anytime. The sooner the better, of course. We'll be here through New Year's, then we'll be back at our town house in the city."

Maggie felt dizzy. Had she really said yes? Mrs. Halvorson thought so. She stood and handed Camille back to her mother, then followed them to the door, her eyes on the pink bonnet.

Maggie closed the door and leaned against it, her eyes closed, her hand clutching her robe. The only sound was the pounding of her heart and it seemed to echo through the house. There was no sound of an ax hitting wood. She froze. She lifted her head and opened her eyes. Garrett stood across the room, leaning against the wall, waiting for her to say something.

"How long have you been there?" Her voice shook.

"Long enough to see you get your baby. You must be very happy."

Three long strides brought him across the floor to face her. "Tell me this, did you hear anything I said last night? Or had you already decided to go?"

The hurt in his eyes made her heart ache, but she couldn't let him know. "I heard you. You fired me, remember?"

"Oh, for heaven's sake, Maggie. It was a shock tactic. It was meant to get your attention. I told you I'd rather have you stay as a nanny than go."

"I also heard you say that you want to get married again and have a baby."

"Yes, I want to get married—to you, and I want to have our baby." His eyes blazed and he grabbed her by the arm.

"And if I let you down?"

"So I'll be let down, and so will you. But we'll be let down together, and we'll try again. And if it turns out we don't have any children, that's okay, too. We have Elliott."

Maggie shook her head. "It won't be okay. I know. I've been through it, you haven't. You wanted a child, you had one. You think it's easy, it probably is for you. But not for me. I can't take the chance of more disappointment. I don't think you can, either. Someday, not this year or next, but someday, maybe when you're old, you'd be sorry and you'd wish you'd waited just a little longer to marry somebody who could have more children for you. And I'd feel even worse because I'd know how much it means to you. You're good at raising things and you want to do it. You ought to be doing it. So by leaving before I've really gotten entrenched in your family, I'm giving you a chance to find somebody else." She pulled her arm away from his.

"I don't want to find somebody else. And if you think you're not entrenched in this family, I don't know what entrenched is. Elliott loves you and I love you. Mrs. Halvorson doesn't love you, and neither does that baby."

Maggie bit her lip to keep from crying. "I admit I've filled a niche in your lives and I think you've mistaken that for love."

"Don't tell me about love, Maggie. You wouldn't know it if you fell over it in the street." He turned on his heel and in seconds she heard the back door slam shut and the sharp sting of the ax against the logs begin again, each one sending a stab of pain into her heart.

She went back to the hot tub, but the water wasn't soothing anymore. And she could still hear the pounding outside. She got dressed and went to the kitchen to make tea and the pounding followed her there and tore her apart. She told herself it would have been worse if she had decided the other way. She was doing what was best for everyone in the long run. But for the short run she was miserable.

At five o'clock Garrett went to pick up Elliott. Maggie made soup and biscuits, but Elliott was the only one who ate. He was the only one who talked, too. Garrett carefully avoided looking at her. He poured her a glass of wine and she looked up to thank him, but closed her mouth when she saw how cold his eyes were.

She wished they could act normally during their last days together, but she realized that was asking too much. As angry as Garrett was, she was surprised he didn't throw her out in the snow. He probably would have if it hadn't been for Elliott.

Elliott and Maggie decorated the tree that evening and Garrett went to the garage to adjust his ski boots. Elliott couldn't hang the strings of popcorn and cranberries on the top of the tree without help, so he went to find Garrett. Maggie felt the wind from the back door as Garrett came in carrying a stepladder with Elliott at his heels giving directions.

"Higher," Elliott called to Garrett who had climbed to the top step and leaned into the tree.

"Like this?" Garrett looked down at Maggie's head beneath him, and gripped the trunk of the tall tree. He wanted to wrap her up in paper chains and strings of cranberries and take her back home with him. He wanted to coax, to beg and to threaten her to stay. But he knew it wouldn't do any good. He knew her stubborn streak. She had made her decision and she was going to stick by it. But that didn't mean he had to make it easy on her.

As soon as the final string of popcorn was in place, Garrett turned on the CD player and played Christmas songs.

"I like the old ones best," he commented, stretching out on the couch on his back. "Don't you, Maggie?"

He hadn't spoken directly to her since his remark about love, and her head jerked up in surprise. She nodded and adjusted the loop of a paper chain on a lower branch of the tree.

"Chestnuts roasting on an open fire," he crooned along with the tape. Elliott laughed and held his hands over his ears.

Maggie smiled, but when the song changed to ''I'll be home for Christmas'' her smile faded and her lips trembled. Garrett turned over and buried his head in the cushions. Let her suffer. She asked for it, he told himself. When he turned over and opened his eyes she was gone.

''Maggie went to bed early,'' Elliott answered his questioning gaze. ''She said she had a hard day.''

''So did I,'' Garrett said. ''Come on, sport, I'll read you a story.''

''I'll ski with Elliott today,'' Garrett told her the next morning at the foot of the chair lift, ''and give you time to yourself, to think things over.''

''I don't need that,'' Maggie protested. Her red ski jacket made a vivid slash against the white slopes behind her; the wind tossed her hair against her cheek.

''That's right.'' He snapped his fingers. ''You've already done it and your mind's made up. Well, I'll give you something to think about. Who's going to tell Elliott, you or me?''

''Me,'' she said quickly, ''but not until after Christmas.'' She looked down at her skis, flexing her boots, ''if that's all right with you. I think he'll understand if I say it right. I've always told him I'd have to leave someday.''

''Maybe he'll take it better than I did,'' he said, unable to control the bitterness in his voice.

She looked up at him, her eyes dark with pain and misery.

He clamped his lips together to keep from saying something he'd regret. ''We'll meet you for lunch down at the barbecue if you want to.''

''Okay.'' Her voice seemed to come from somewhere deep inside her, and he couldn't stand there anymore watching her suffer, even if it was her own fault.

The next morning they went shopping. Maggie went to the grocery store to buy the turkey for Christmas dinner and Garrett headed down the street toward the stationery store.

The hours until Christmas snowballed into each other, until on Christmas morning Maggie sat cold and numb next to Elliott on the floor and watched his face glow with excitement. She was wearing her warmest sweater, but nothing could stop the chill from creeping in around her heart.

"Maggie." Elliott crawled under the tree and reached for a round cylinder wrapped in construction paper. "Open mine first."

She felt Garrett standing behind her and she willed her voice to be steady. For Elliott's sake, she told herself, make this a happy day.

"I don't know what it could be," she exclaimed, shaking the paper scroll.

"I made it at school," he explained, the excitement in his eyes magnified by his glasses.

She opened the package and unrolled a stiff cardboard with a small handprint on it. Underneath the blue hand impression she read the words out loud.

"This is my hand so tiny and small,
For you to hang upon the wall
For you to watch as the years go by
How we grew, my hand and I."

Maggie stopped and held her breath. She wouldn't cry. She would *not* cry. Not now. Not yet.

"Do you like it?" Elliott demanded, watching her face.

"I love it. I'm going to hang it on the wall, just like it says."

"Good."

"There's one for you under there, Elliott," she said, her throat aching.

He set to work ripping paper, tearing boxes and laughing with surprise and delight. Garrett had spent both time and money on Elliott. Maggie shouldn't have been surprised at that but she was. Elliott put his jacket on and went outside to test a remote-control tank that Garrett had given him.

Maggie walked across the room and sat on the floor. She leaned back against the couch and stretched her feet out in front of her. It was almost over. Only one more hurdle.

"There's a present for you under the tree, Garrett," she said quickly before she lost her nerve.

"For me, really?" He sounded about as interested as if she'd said there was a hole in his sock.

She nodded, unable to speak any more around the lump in her throat.

He got up out of his chair next to the fireplace where he was burning old wrapping paper and went down on his knees to reach for one of the two remaining packages.

"And here's one for you." He pushed it to her across the carpet, and she looked up.

"Don't worry," he assured her. "It's not a nightgown. It's just what you told me to get." He looked down at the package in his hands. "And I'm sure you got me something just as appropriate, right out of the nanny's handbook." His voice was carefully cool and impersonal.

She gripped the square box he'd given her tightly and looked at him. "Well, not exactly. It's something I made myself, and it's probably not...well, go ahead and open it."

"Made it yourself?" He fumbled with the ribbon. "What is it, a fruitcake?" He looked down at the sweater without moving and without talking for such a long time Maggie began to wonder what was wrong. He couldn't have seen the mistakes in it yet. He couldn't know if the sleeves were too long. She tugged nervously at her own sleeves.

"What is it?" she asked finally, standing up and walking over to him. Maybe he didn't like green. Come to think of it, she'd never seen him wear anything green before. Or maybe he was allergic to wool. Why hadn't she used the yarn to make that scarf for her grandmother?

"It's a sweater," he said in a choked voice. "You made me a sweater." He looked up at her, his mouth twisted in a grimace. "No one ever made anything for me before."

"It might not fit," she suggested, giving him a way out. If he didn't like it he wouldn't ever have to wear it. He could just say it didn't fit. Why didn't he say it? Why didn't he say something?

He stood up and held it against his shoulders. His face showed no emotion at all.

"Hold your arms up," she told him, taking the sweater out of his hands with shaking fingers.

He raised his arms above his head, and she pulled the sweater over his head brushing her fingers awkwardly against his hair and his chest. The sleeves hung down and covered his hands. She shook her head. She should have measured his arms. But she'd been right about the color. The green made his eyes look brighter, and she stumbled back to escape the heat of his gaze.

"The sleeves are too long," she said finally just to break the silence.

"I can roll them up."

Suddenly her anxiety reached the breaking point. "Do you like it?" she blurted.

He nodded solemnly. "Yeah, I do." His eyes met hers and the smallest suggestion of a smile played at his lips.

Her heart lifted. He liked it. She exhaled slowly. Maybe he really would wear it and think of her when he felt the warmth of the wool against his body. "Well, I've got to put the turkey in the oven."

"Wait a minute, you forgot your present."

She sat on the edge of the couch and opened the package as fast as Elliott had opened his. A dark red leather desk calendar lay inside the box. She breathed a sigh of relief.

"This is perfect." She smoothed the wrinkles from the tissue paper around the calendar. "How did you know what I wanted?"

"Look inside at the pages."

She turned the faintly lined pages and saw that Garrett had written on some of the blank spaces under the dates. She thumbed through and stopped at March 5. "Elliott's birthday," he had written. On September 6 there was another scrawl, "The day you came to our house." The lump in her throat was back. She couldn't look up, couldn't meet his eyes.

She turned some more pages. "October 31, Halloween. Where are you Maggie, whose fortune are you telling?" A tear trickled down her cheek and onto the page blurring the letters. She could almost smell the pumpkins, taste the apples, feel Garrett's lips on hers. That was what he intended, writing on the calendar like this. She looked up.

He was watching her closely. "You said a calendar was all right, but I can see you don't like it. Don't worry." He reached into his back pocket and held a small package in his hand. "It comes with an eraser. You can erase all the things I wrote. Just the way you're going to erase all the memories of the last few months."

Maggie shook her head. "I can't do that. I don't want to do that. I . . . I've enjoyed these last months. I'll never forget them."

Garrett stuffed the eraser back into his pocket and held out his hand.

"Well, we've enjoyed them, too, Maggie," he said, mocking her politeness, "and we wish you the best of luck."

"Thank you." Maggie pointedly ignored his sarcasm and pretended to accept his words at face value. She extended her hand but instead of shaking it he pulled her roughly into his arms and kissed her with a passion she'd never felt before. It was hello and goodbye and bitter regrets all mixed together in one kiss. She stumbled back and fell onto the couch next to her desk calendar. She pressed her fingers against her lips, shocked and shaken to her toes.

"Just something to remember me by, in case you lose the calendar," he said before he stalked out of the living room.

The rest of the day passed in a blur. The smell of the turkey roasting, the empty feeling in the pit of her stomach. A subdued Garrett carving the turkey as carefully as if they had a house full of guests. Elliott playing with his new toys oblivious to the tension around him. And the feeling of dread that dogged her until she dropped from fatigue into the water bed.

The next day Garrett promised to pack her things at home and send them to her. She said she'd come and get them herself. He said no and she said yes. It occurred to her that he didn't want to see her again, and she gave in.

"I know Mrs. Newcastle will find you another nanny. Someone older and more mature. The type you were looking for. She owes it to you," Maggie suggested, leaning against the kitchen counter.

"She owes me a lot more than that."

Maggie flushed. Garrett turned to the stove and poured himself a cup of coffee. "I don't need a nanny anymore, thanks. I'm going to stay home for a while. I can't do much at the river during the winter anyway. So you see, your timing was perfect."

"Your timing. You fired me."

"I'll take it back if you say so." Garrett's voice was steady, but his coffee cup rattled against the tile counter.

"It's too late." Maggie turned on her heel and went into the living room to say goodbye to Elliott.

She found him lying under the Christmas tree with the model brontosaurus she'd given him.

She stooped down next to him. When she told him she was going to leave he blinked behind his thick glasses.

"Just like Mary Poppins left the Banks family," he said matter-of-factly.

"That's right." She looked at him carefully, holding her breath. She thought he might cry, she thought he might be mad at her, but she didn't expect him to take it so well.

"I'm glad you gave me this brontosaurus then, Maggie, because he reminds me of you."

"Me?" The tears sprang to Maggie's eyes and she turned her head away. "Why?"

"Because brontosaurus is your favorite dinosaur," he reminded her. "Did you forget?"

"No, of course not." Maggie's face was wet now, the tears were falling thick and fast. The more he held his feelings in check, the more she came apart. "I have to go now. We had a good time together, Elliott.... I...I..."

Maggie jumped up and ran out of the room. She bumped into Garrett on her way to the door, but he made no effort to stop her or to say goodbye. She grabbed her small suitcase and her jacket and ran down the path to the waiting car.

Chapter Eleven

It wasn't fair of Maggie to compare conditions at the Halvorsons' tall Georgian brick town house with those at the trout farm. And for the first few weeks, Maggie didn't try. She was busy learning a new routine of appointments and birthday parties and sessions at the kindergym. She took care of the baby and tried not to think about a boy and a man in an old house by the side of the road with a sign out in front saying, "Everyone Catches One."

It was true—the Halvorsons had a very active social life and they did seem to know all the right people. Mrs. Newcastle had been right about that. But Maggie found the right people were the wrong people for her.

"Let's face it," she told the baby one afternoon on their way to the park on the top of the hill. "I'm not exactly the greatest company these days." The baby drooled.

"The right people are nice enough," she continued. "I'm the one who doesn't seem quite right."

Actually Maggie knew she was as right as she could be under the circumstances, as well as reliable and dependable, everything a nanny should be, and the Halvorsons had nothing to complain about. How could they know that the spark that made her a great nanny instead of just a good nanny had gone out?

That afternoon Mrs. Halvorson paused in the spacious nursery with a view of the bay and gave Maggie a long, worried look.

"Is anything wrong?" she asked, giving the baby a kiss on the cheek and handing her back to Maggie.

Maggie looked into the baby's face with concern.

"I mean with you," Mrs. Halvorson explained.

"Oh, no, I'm fine," Maggie said quickly. "Is there something I'm not doing right?"

Mrs. Halvorson gave a faint smile. "Eating, for one thing. You look as if you'd lost ten pounds since you've been here. The other day when you joined us for lunch you hardly touched your soufflé. You're not allergic to eggs, are you?"

Maggie held the baby to her shoulder to block her face.

"No, I'm not. And I really haven't lost ten pounds." More like twelve, she thought. She couldn't explain about the knot in her stomach that wouldn't go away. The awful feeling of loss whenever she thought about the other half of her life going on some hundred miles away without her.

"Mrs. Newcastle called me yesterday. She's very anxious to know how you're adjusting. If you're meeting people and so on. I told her that at our party the other night—"

"I know," Maggie interrupted. "I left early. I appreciate your inviting me. It's just that it's taking me a little longer to adjust than I thought, from the place where I was to this." Maggie gestured with her free hand at the softly carpeted nursery with the patterned wallpaper and matching curtains.

Mrs. Halvorson nodded understandingly. "Mrs. Newcastle told me about the situation at the trout farm. No free time, no one to talk to, a ramshackle house without even the barest amenities." She sighed sympathetically. "No won-

der it's taking you a while to adjust. Just take your time and
do whatever feels right to you.''

Maggie smiled ruefully. ''Thank you, but...'' She
stopped. She couldn't tell her that she didn't need free time,
that she'd had two people to talk to and that all the amenities of life seemed to be contained right inside that old ramshackle house. Love was there and Maggie missed it more
than she let herself think.

Not that there wasn't love in the Halvorson house. There
was. But Maggie wasn't a part of it and she never would be.
She had complained often enough to Garrett that he didn't
treat her like a nanny, but now that she was treated like one
she realized that she didn't want to be, after all. She pre-
ferred to be treated as an equal and as a woman, the way
Garrett had treated her from the first day she arrived. She
held the baby's cheek next to hers and shed a tear for what
she had had and what she'd lost.

Think of what you've done for Garrett, she reminded
herself, trying to feel noble. He's probably found somebody by now, a nanny or a potential mother for his children or both. And if she hadn't left when she did, he never
would have.

Mrs. Halvorson was standing at the door, waiting for
Maggie to speak and adjusting her scarf at her throat.

''Speaking of the trout farm,'' Maggie said lightly, ''did
Mrs. Newcastle say anything about sending a new nanny to
the farm? I've been worried about leaving them in the
lurch...I just wondered...''

Mrs. Halvorson paused with her hand on the doorknob.
''I believe she offered to replace you at no extra charge, but
Mr., uh, Mr.—''

''Townsend.''

''Mr. Townsend told her that nobody could take your
place. Now that was nice, wasn't it? You can't get a better
recommendation than that.''

Maggie nodded and Mrs. Halvorson blew a kiss to the
baby and closed the door behind her.

* * *

On her way to the park the next morning Maggie bought a newspaper and read it on the park bench while Camille slept in the shade in her adjustable stroller. There were a dozen ads for nannies, but only one interested her. It said, "Wanted, twenty-eight-year-old nanny with previous experience on trout farm. Must be kind, patient, loving, helpful and understanding." The address of a post office box in San Gregorio was included for replies.

Maggie folded the newspaper with trembling hands. She looked down at the baby, who was oblivious to her nanny, and turmoil bubbled inside her. She thought about Mrs. Halvorson with her busy life filled with charity balls and community good works.

She thought about leaving and wondered how it would look on her résumé, two jobs in six months. She felt the wall of protests she'd given Garrett crumbling around her. It was time to admit to herself that being a nanny was not as fulfilling as she had hoped it would be. It was a noble profession, but it was not for her. Not now, not anymore. For her it had become a substitute for being a wife and mother.

The words in the advertisement ran through her mind as she walked briskly back to the Halvorsons', past restored Victorian houses and tall apartment buildings with doormen. If only she could get there before somebody else got the job. She smiled to herself. Who else was qualified?

After dinner Maggie sat in the bedroom of her suite, which adjoined the nursery, and restlessly leafed through the calendar Garrett had given her for Christmas. Many pages were blank in the spring; since she hadn't been on the farm last spring there were no memories attached to the dates.

But on April 12, a Saturday, Garrett had drawn two bells touching each other. Wedding bells? Maggie's heart raced. She paced back and forth, then went downstairs to give the Halvorsons two weeks' notice.

They were puzzled but gracious. And Mrs. Newcastle came through with another nanny for them before Maggie had even packed her bags. Who wouldn't want to live in a separate wing with a view of the bay, two days off a week and an adorable baby to take care of?

But Maggie had no regrets, no fears, no backward glances until she drove up to the farmhouse that rainy day and saw Garrett's truck parked out in front. Then she almost turned around and went back to the highway to telephone first. Maybe he already had a new nanny. Maybe the ad was a joke. He couldn't really believe that she'd read it and come back, could he? Yes, she smiled to herself, he could.

She parked in front of the house, looked at her pale, thin face in the rearview mirror and felt the panic rise in her throat. She tightened the belt on her raincoat and ran through the softly falling raindrops to the front steps of the house. The front door opened and Garrett stood on the porch wearing the sweater she'd made him for Christmas. She'd seen him try on the sweater, but she'd never actually seen him wear it. He had pushed the long sleeves up over the elbows and she stared at the muscles in his forearms, at his shoulders and his chest while the memories came flooding back. The first day she arrived, with him standing on the porch just as he was now. The day he kissed her, that warm, ripe Indian summer morning, tasting of coffee and smelling like hay fields and fresh river water.

But this was different. A cold rain was falling and Garrett was standing there waiting for her to speak. With her eyes she pleaded with him to help her out, to give her another chance to say yes.

Garrett finally broke the silence. "What are you doing here?" He leaned as casually as he could against the door frame and looked down at her. He was surprised at how steady his voice sounded when his whole body felt strung out as tight as the fence wire that surrounded the property.

Maggie pulled her collar up around her face. The rain was running off the roof and onto her hair. He took a step forward. He wanted to cover her head with his hands, cover her mouth with his and bring her inside where she belonged. But she didn't belong there anymore. And if he did that he was letting himself in for more pain. And he'd had enough pain these past six weeks to last a lifetime.

"I was just passing through the neighborhood," Maggie said lightly, "so I thought I'd stop by and see how Elliott was doing."

Her cheekbones made her face seem all angles, and there were dark smudges under her eyes. Rain dripped off her forehead and fell down her cheeks like tears. His chest tightened. His mind told him to keep her out of his house and out of his life. But his heart took over.

"Would you like to come in out of the rain?" he asked, unable to stop staring at her. Yes, he'd put the ad in the paper, yes, he'd hoped she'd answer it, but that was days ago, days of waiting by the phone. And now she was here, but he didn't know why.

She walked up the steps and he held the door open for her. Out of habit they walked to the kitchen and Maggie stood at the table looking around. He watched her eyes rove over the cabinets and spice shelf and the refrigerator where Elliott's latest drawing was attached with a magnet. She gave a little shiver.

He frowned. "You're soaking wet. Take off your coat. I'll get you a towel." He went to the bathroom and when he returned she had draped her coat over the back of the chair and was sitting down with her head propped in her hands. He walked up behind her and put his hands on her temples. He wound the towel around her hair and rubbed it gently between his fingers.

She closed her eyes and leaned back against him. The touch of her head against his stomach sent a jolt of electricity through his body. An uneven ragged sigh escaped from her lips.

If he leaned down just a few more inches he could kiss her and she wouldn't resist, he could tell by the way her cheeks flushed and by her breathing. But there were things he had to find out first.

He quickened the pace of his hands on her hair and when her hair was dry he folded the towel and walked over to the stove.

Maggie stifled a cry of protest. Don't stop, she wanted to say. Every fiber of her body wanted his hands on her.

"Would you like a cup of coffee?" he asked. Maggie nodded mutely. She watched while he poured hot water through a filter into a cup.

"Aren't you going to have some?" she asked.

"I don't drink coffee anymore. It keeps me awake."

"Even in the morning?" She looked closely at his face and saw lines around his eyes that hadn't been there before. If it wasn't coffee, then something else was keeping him awake.

"Anytime. But it doesn't seem to matter. I can't sleep, anyway." He set her coffee in front of her. "Why did you come, Maggie? Did you come about the job?"

"I'm not looking for a job. You want a lot in a nanny, and I don't think I qualify." She took a deep breath. "Anyway, I don't want to be a nanny anymore."

"What?" He sat down across the table from her and his eyes bored holes in her.

"I quit my job." She laughed nervously. "I know, it doesn't look very good, does it? Fired after three months on my first job, then quitting the next one after only six weeks."

"What do you want to be?" He held his breath and the only sound was the rain splattering against the kitchen window. He wanted to reach out for her and hold her face in his hands and kiss her and never let her go. Instead he tilted his chair back and gripped the seat.

"I . . . I don't know. I thought I'd see what was available." She searched his face for a sign, some indication that he still felt the way he did before Christmas, but his jaw seemed to be locked into place, his eyes watching her. She forced herself to speak. "I had a good offer a few months ago. I turned it down. I think I made a mistake."

"What makes you think that? You were pretty sure of yourself when you walked out."

Maggie's lips trembled. She had hurt Garrett more than she realized. If she thought she could just walk back into the farmhouse, into his life, she was mistaken. Her throat ached with the fear that he didn't want her anymore.

"No, no, I wasn't. I had to act that way to convince myself to go. But I don't want to take care of other people's children anymore. I want to take care of my own, if I can have any. And if not..." she trailed off. Garrett was watching her closely. "If not . . . I'll make the best of it."

Maggie stood up and walked around the table. "I thought I was being noble and unselfish by leaving you. But I couldn't live with my noble, unselfish self. I couldn't live without...without you." Her voice broke then. "I've missed you so much." She put her hand on his shoulder and he covered it with his.

He stood and pulled her to him. She felt lighter and thinner against him, but still soft and warm and still Maggie. He'd put the ad in the newspaper, but he hadn't really thought she'd come. Happiness surged through his body and relief so strong he couldn't speak.

"I was looking at my calendar," she said, her voice muffled against his chest, "and I saw something that looked like bells on April 12."

"Is that right?" He kissed her hair and her forehead and his lips trailed a path down to her throat. "Those were wedding bells. The grass should be in along the river by then. I reserved a spot above the north fork." He tilted her chin and kissed her on the mouth, long and deep, the way she'd dreamed of since the first day she'd arrived. His arms closed around her and their bodies melted together.

When Maggie pulled away, breathless and light-headed, she looked into his dark eyes and swayed back against his chest.

"I told you once I thought it would be wonderful to be married to you. But you told me I wouldn't know what love was if I fell over it in the street," she reminded him.

"I was wrong." He grinned at her with a lopsided grin. "I wouldn't marry anybody who couldn't recognize love."

"No, you were right. I did fall over it in the street, the first day I came here, and I didn't recognize it—until I came back today. It's still out there." She looked around the kitchen and sighed with happiness. "It's in here, too. It's everywhere you are."

He corrected her gently. "It's everywhere we are."

Epilogue

Christmas, Two Years Later

Mrs. Newcastle was hanging the last of the glass ornaments on the desktop Christmas tree when the mailman slid a fistful of last-minute Christmas cards through the mail slot at the prestigious school for nannies. She drew a letter opener from her desk drawer and carefully slit the top of a large red envelope with a Lake Tahoe postmark.

When she opened the card a color snapshot fell out. Mrs. Newcastle reached for her glasses and gazed intently at a photograph of what appeared to be an all-American family. A tall man with a shock of dark hair was holding a dark-haired, pink-cheeked baby girl and a woman had her arm around a seven-year-old boy with glasses.

Mrs. Newcastle found herself smiling at the family portrait. It was most unusual, highly irregular and definitely against the rules for any of her girls to marry an employer. But once in a while—not very often, thank heavens—it did happen. And when it did, Mrs. Newcastle was the first to admit she'd been wrong.

She turned in her swivel chair to face the motto on the wall behind the desk. "See the World with the Rich and Famous." She might have to alter that sign one of these days. She might have to add, "Or stay home and let the world come to you." The picture of Maggie's radiant face told her that she would agree with that.

*   *   *   *   *

COMING NEXT MONTH

#694 ETHAN—Diana Palmer—A Diamond Jubilee Title!
Don't miss *Ethan*—he's one Long, Tall Texan who'll have your heart roped and tied!

#695 GIVEAWAY GIRL—Val Whisenand
Private investigator Mike Dixon never meant to fall in love with Amy Alexander. How could he possibly tell her the painful truth about her mysterious past?

#696 JAKE'S CHILD—Lindsay Longford
The moment Jake Donnelly arrived with a bedraggled child, Sarah Jane Simpson felt a strange sense of foreboding. Could the little boy be her long-lost son?

#697 DEARLY BELOVED—Jane Bierce
Rebecca Hobbs thought a visit to her sleepy southern hometown would be restful. But handsome minister Frank Andrews had her heart working overtime!

#698 HONEYMOON HIDEAWAY—Linda Varner
Divorce lawyer Sam Knight was convinced that true love was a myth. But Libby Turner, a honeymoon hideaway manager, was set to prove him wrong with one kiss as evidence....

#699 NO HORSING AROUND—Stella Bagwell
Jacqui Prescott was determined to show cynical Spencer Matlock she was a capable jockey. But then she found herself suddenly longing to come in first in the sexy trainer's heart!

AVAILABLE THIS MONTH:

#688 FATHER CHRISTMAS
Mary Blayney

#689 DREAM AGAIN OF LOVE
Phyllis Halldorson

#690 MAKE ROOM FOR NANNY
Carol Grace

#691 MAKESHIFT MARRIAGE
Janet Franklin

#692 TEN DAYS IN PARADISE
Karen Leabo

#693 SWEET ADELINE
Sharon De Vita

DIAMOND JUBILEE CELEBRATION!

It's Silhouette Books' tenth anniversary, and what better way to celebrate than to toast *you*, our readers, for making it all possible. Each month in 1990, we'll present you with a DIAMOND JUBILEE Silhouette Romance written by an all-time favorite author!

Welcome the new year with *Ethan*—a LONG, TALL TEXANS book by Diana Palmer. February brings Brittany Young's *The Ambassador's Daughter*. Look for *Never on Sundae* by Rita Rainville in March, and in April you'll find *Harvey's Missing* by Peggy Webb. Victoria Glenn, Lucy Gordon, Annette Broadrick, Dixie Browning and many more have special gifts of love waiting for you with their DIAMOND JUBILEE Romances.

Be sure to look for the distinctive DIAMOND JUBILEE emblem, and share in Silhouette's celebration. Saying thanks has never been so romantic. . . .

Silhouette Romances

**Diana Palmer brings you an Award of Excellence
title . . . and the first Silhouette Romance DIAMOND
JUBILEE book.**

ETHAN
by Diana Palmer

This month, Diana Palmer continues her bestselling
LONG, TALL TEXANS series with *Ethan*—the story
of a rugged rancher who refuses to get roped and tied
by Arabella Craig, the one woman he can't resist.

The Award of Excellence is given to one
specially selected title per month. Spend
January with *Ethan* #694 . . . a special
DIAMOND JUBILEE title . . . only in
Silhouette Romance.

Ethan-1

You'll flip . . . your pages won't!
Read paperbacks *hands-free* with

Book Mate · I

The perfect "mate" for all your romance paperbacks

**Traveling • Vacationing • At Work • In Bed • Studying
• Cooking • Eating**

Perfect size for all standard paperbacks, this wonderful invention makes reading a pure pleasure! Ingenious design holds paperback books OPEN and FLAT so even wind can't ruffle pages — leaves your hands free to do other things. Reinforced, wipe-clean vinyl-covered holder flexes to let you turn pages without undoing the strap . . . supports paperbacks so well, they have the strength of hardcovers!

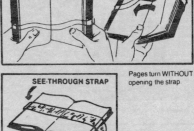

Pages turn WITHOUT opening the strap.

SEE-THROUGH STRAP

Reinforced back stays flat.

Built in bookmark

BOOK MARK

BACK COVER HOLDING STRIP

10″ x 7¼″, opened.
Snaps closed for easy carrying, too.

INDULGE A LITTLE SWEEPSTAKES

OFFICIAL RULES

SWEEPSTAKES RULES AND REGULATIONS. NO PURCHASE NECESSARY.

1. NO PURCHASE NECESSARY. To enter complete the official entry form and return with the invoice in the envelope provided. Or you may enter by printing your name, complete address and your daytime phone number on a 3 x 5 piece of paper. Include with your entry the hand printed words "Indulge A Little Sweepstakes." Mail your entry to: Indulge A Little Sweepstakes, P.O. Box 1397, Buffalo, NY 14269-1397. No mechanically reproduced entries accepted. Not responsible for late, lost, misdirected mail, or printing errors.

2. Three winners, one per month (Sept. 30, 1989, October 31, 1989 and November 30, 1989), will be selected in random drawings. All entries received prior to the drawing date will be eligible for that month's prize. This sweepstakes is under the supervision of MARDEN-KANE, INC. an independent judging organization whose decisions are final and binding. Winners will be notified by telephone and may be required to execute an affidavit of eligibility and release which must be returned within 14 days, or an alternate winner will be selected.

3. Prizes: 1st Grand Prize (1) a trip for two to Disneyworld in Orlando, Florida. Trip includes round trip air transportation, hotel accommodations for seven days and six nights, plus up to $700 expense money (ARV $3,500). 2nd Grand Prize (1) a seven-night Chandris Caribbean Cruise for two includes transportation from nearest major airport, accommodations, meals plus up to $1,000 in expense money (ARV $4,300). 3rd Grand Prize (1) a ten-day Hawaiian holiday for two includes round trip air transportation for two, hotel accommodations, sightseeing, plus up to $1,200 in spending money (ARV $7,700). All trips subject to availability and must be taken as outlined on the entry form.

4. Sweepstakes open to residents of the U.S. and Canada 18 years or older except employees and the families of Torstar Corp., its affiliates, subsidiaries and Marden-Kane, Inc. and all other agencies and persons connected with conducting this sweepstakes. All Federal, State and local laws and regulations apply. Void wherever prohibited or restricted by law. Taxes, if any are the sole responsibility of the prize winners. Canadian winners will be required to answer a skill testing question. Winners consent to the use of their name, photograph and/or likeness for publicity purposes without additional compensation.

5. For a list of prize winners, send a stamped, self-addressed envelope to Indulge A Little Sweepstakes Winners, P.O. Box 701, Sayreville, NJ 08871.

© 1989 HARLEQUIN ENTERPRISES LTD.   DL-SWPS

INDULGE A LITTLE SWEEPSTAKES

OFFICIAL RULES

SWEEPSTAKES RULES AND REGULATIONS. NO PURCHASE NECESSARY.

1. NO PURCHASE NECESSARY. To enter complete the official entry form and return with the invoice in the envelope provided. Or you may enter by printing your name, complete address and your daytime phone number on a 3 x 5 piece of paper. Include with your entry the hand printed words "Indulge A Little Sweepstakes." Mail your entry to: Indulge A Little Sweepstakes, P.O. Box 1397, Buffalo, NY 14269-1397. No mechanically reproduced entries accepted. Not responsible for late, lost, misdirected mail, or printing errors.

2. Three winners, one per month (Sept. 30, 1989, October 31, 1989 and November 30, 1989), will be selected in random drawings. All entries received prior to the drawing date will be eligible for that month's prize. This sweepstakes is under the supervision of MARDEN-KANE, INC. an independent judging organization whose decisions are final and binding. Winners will be notified by telephone and may be required to execute an affidavit of eligibility and release which must be returned within 14 days, or an alternate winner will be selected.

3. Prizes: 1st Grand Prize (1) a trip for two to Disneyworld in Orlando, Florida. Trip includes round trip air transportation, hotel accommodations for seven days and six nights, plus up to $700 expense money (ARV $3,500). 2nd Grand Prize (1) a seven-night Chandris Caribbean Cruise for two includes transportation from nearest major airport, accommodations, meals plus up to $1,000 in expense money (ARV $4,300). 3rd Grand Prize (1) a ten-day Hawaiian holiday for two includes round trip air transportation for two, hotel accommodations, sightseeing, plus up to $1,200 in spending money (ARV $7,700). All trips subject to availability and must be taken as outlined on the entry form.

4. Sweepstakes open to residents of the U.S. and Canada 18 years or older except employees and the families of Torstar Corp., its affiliates, subsidiaries and Marden-Kane, Inc. and all other agencies and persons connected with conducting this sweepstakes. All Federal, State and local laws and regulations apply. Void wherever prohibited or restricted by law. Taxes, if any are the sole responsibility of the prize winners. Canadian winners will be required to answer a skill testing question. Winners consent to the use of their name, photograph and/or likeness for publicity purposes without additional compensation.

5. For a list of prize winners, send a stamped, self-addressed envelope to Indulge A Little Sweepstakes Winners, P.O. Box 701, Sayreville, NJ 08871.

© 1989 HARLEQUIN ENTERPRISES LTD.   DL-SWPS

INDULGE A LITTLE—WIN A LOT!

Summer of '89 Subscribers-Only Sweepstakes

OFFICIAL ENTRY FORM

This entry must be received by: Nov. 30, 1989
This month's winner will be notified by: Dec. 7, 1989
Trip must be taken between: Jan. 7, 1990–Jan. 7, 1991

YES, I want to win the 3-Island Hawaiian vacation for two! I understand the prize includes round-trip airfare, first-class hotels, and a daily allowance as revealed on the "Wallet" scratch-off card.

Name_____

Address_____

City_____ State/Prov._____ Zip/Postal Code_____

Daytime phone number_____
                                          Area code

Return entries with invoice in envelope provided. Each book in this shipment has two entry coupons—and the more coupons you enter, the better your chances of winning!
© 1989 HARLEQUIN ENTERPRISES LTD.

DINDL-3

INDULGE A LITTLE—WIN A LOT!

Summer of '89 Subscribers-Only Sweepstakes

OFFICIAL ENTRY FORM

This entry must be received by: Nov. 30, 1989
This month's winner will be notified by: Dec. 7, 1989
Trip must be taken between: Jan. 7, 1990–Jan. 7, 1991

YES, I want to win the 3-Island Hawaiian vacation for two! I understand the prize includes round-trip airfare, first-class hotels, and a daily allowance as revealed on the "Wallet" scratch-off card.

Name_____

Address_____

City_____ State/Prov._____ Zip/Postal Code_____

Daytime phone number_____
                                          Area code

Return entries with invoice in envelope provided. Each book in this shipment has two entry coupons—and the more coupons you enter, the better your chances of winning!
© 1989 HARLEQUIN ENTERPRISES LTD.

DINDL-3